I0679563

# UNDERCOVER MIAMI

## A CLIFF FORD MYSTERY

*Terry Toler*

*Undercover Miami*
Published by: BeHoldings, LLC

Copyright ©2025, **BeHoldings, LLC**
**Terry Toler**
*All Rights Reserved*

All rights reserved. No part of this publication may be reproduced, stored in a retrieval system, or transmitted in any form, or by any means—electronic, mechanical, photocopying, recording or otherwise—without prior written permission.

Book Cover: BeHoldings Publishing
Editor: Jeanne Leach
Contributing Editor: Donna Toler

For information email: terry@terrytoler.com.

Our books can be purchased in bulk for promotional, educational, and business use. Please contact your bookseller or the BeHoldings Publishing Sales department at: sales@terrytoler.com

For booking information email: booking@terrytoler.com.
First U.S. Edition: May 2025
Printed in the United States of America
ISBN Paperback 978-1-954710-27-6

This is a work of fiction. All of the characters, organizations, and events portrayed in this novel are either products of the author's imagination or are used fictitiously. Any resemblance to actual persons, living or dead, is entirely coincidental.

# OTHER BOOKS BY TERRY TOLER

## Fiction

The Longest Day

The Reformation of Mars

The Late, Great Planet Jupiter

The Great Wall of Ven-Us

Saturn: The Eden Experiment

The Mercury Protocols

The Heart of Pluto

Save The Girls

The Ingenue

Saving Sara

Save The Queen

No Girl Left Behind

The Launch

Body Count

Save Me Twice

Powerful Enemies

Deadly Games

Don't Be Careful

Wintervention

Saving Alex

Forsaken

Fugitives

Cliff Hangers: Anna

Cliff Hangers: Mr. & Mrs. Platt

Cliff Hangers: The Quarterback

Cliff Hangers: Macy

Cliff Hangers: Not, Not Guilty

The Blue Rose

Triggers

For more information on these books and other resources visit
terrytoler.com.

Thank you for purchasing this novel from best-selling author, Terry Toler. As an additional thank you, Terry wants to give you a free gift.

Sign up for:

*Updates*
*New Releases*
*Announcements*

At terrytoler.com

We'll send you an eBook, *The Book Club*, a Cliff Hangers novella, free of charge.

*For my Aunt Shirley*

# 1

For the first time in her life, Allison Mansfield held a gun in her hand intending to use it.

The air was thick with eerie silence in the palatial mansion on Prosper Lane, interrupted only by the soft footsteps as she ascended the left side of the curved grand staircases which would've dominated the entryway if not for the massive chandelier that hung in splendor from the ceiling.

Why the left side? Perhaps because she was left-handed. Maybe because her husband Grimes always took the right. The two were opposites in every way.

Her heart pounded in her chest, and each beat echoed in her ears like a distant drum. The weight of the gun felt foreign, yet somehow fated. Several times she feared dropping it; that's how hard her left hand shook.

Turning back wasn't an option, so she willed herself to take each step until she made it to the landing, then continued down the long hallway to the master bedroom. Pausing outside their bedroom door, her right hand trembled as she reached for the polished-brass handle purchased during one of their trips to Italy.

One of the few things in the twenty-three-thousand-square-foot house Grimes had allowed her to pick out when they built it.

She took a deep breath, steadying herself while slowly opening the door. The bedroom was a picture of luxury, adorned with silk drapes and filled with antique furniture she hated, passed down through generations on his side of the family.

A large portrait of Grimes's mother hung above the bed. Something she despised almost as much as the woman herself.

The bathroom light Grimes insisted stay on all night cast an eerie shadow over the room but gave her what she needed. Things seemed peaceful, a stark contrast to the turmoil brewing within her.

Allison stepped inside, her footsteps muffled by the plush carpet, although unimportant since Grimes was a heavy sleeper. Within seconds, she stood at the side of the bed even though she didn't remember walking over there.

There lay Grimes in his usual position—sleeping on his back, mouth hanging open, oblivious to what was about to happen. The thought occurred to her that it'd be easier if Grimes slept on his stomach, so she wouldn't have to see his face.

His expression would now be frozen in time, forever etched in her memory.

Unexpectedly, memories of their life together flashed before her eyes—extravagant parties, exotic vacations, one no-limit credit card she used to fill her lavish closet and buy whatever else she wanted whenever she wanted it.

What became foremost in her mind in that contemplative moment was the endless facade of empty smiles and hollow laughter. Tears formed in her eyes, but she fought them back. The image of a perfect life was crumbling, revealing the cracks that had been there all along.

The pretense of happiness.

She lifted the gun, her hand steadier now as a steely resolve took hold, fueled by a deep anger that had led her to retrieve it from her husband's office safe. Maybe sleeping on his back was better after all. Seeing his face had reignited the rage that had brought her to this moment in time and gave her the confidence to continue with her premeditated plan.

She aimed at his chest, her finger hovering over the trigger. She'd played this moment in her mind a thousand times.

*Don't aim for the head. You might miss. He could wake up and take the gun from you.*

2

What she hadn't expected was how it felt. Time seemed to stand still as she grappled with the burden of her decision which pressed down on her like a heavy weight sitting on her chest.

Before the doubts could gain root, a single shot rang out, shattering the silence. Grimes's body jerked once, then lay still. The scent of gunpowder filled the room mixed with the metallic smell of blood.

Immediately followed by a scream that escaped from the back of her throat.

She fired a second shot that found its mark.

Allison stood frozen, struggling to process what she'd done. The gun slipped from her hand and landed heavily on the carpet with a thud. She stumbled backwards, her breath coming in panic-attack-like gasps.

With her entire body trembling, she took two hesitant steps forward and reached out to touch the side of his neck. Her fingers were met with an icy chill.

No pulse. Definitely dead.

The tears were suddenly gone.

Fumbling for the phone in her pocket, her fingers felt numb and clumsy. But dialing 911 somehow gave her a sense of closure. Acceptance. The operator's voice on the other end of the line was calm, almost detached, mirroring how she felt. Devoid of any emotion at all.

"911, what's your emergency?"

"I just killed my husband." Allison's voice was barely a whisper, as her tone reflected the gravity of her actions no normal person would understand without knowing the unspeakable secrets she'd take with her to prison.

The words lingered and an awkward pause ensued before the operator's voice came back sharp and urgent. "Ma'am, where are you right now?"

"At home," Allison replied, her voice growing steadier as confidence replaced the fear. "At our house on Prosper Lane." She blurted out the address even though the lady didn't ask for it.

"Is anyone else in the house with you?" the operator asked.

Allison shook her head, though she knew the operator couldn't see her. "No, just me and him."

She turned her back to the lifeless body on the bed, no longer able to look at the man who had captured her heart years ago and had twisted the goodwill into a pile of bitterness, shame, and animosity. Bringing out the worst in her.

"Stay on the line, Ma'am. Help is on the way."

Allison sank to the floor in the corner of the room and waited for the police to arrive. It didn't seem appropriate to sit on the chaise lounge Grimes had picked out and paid for, even though it's the only piece of furniture in the room she loved.

The last few minutes played in her mind like a movie in a theater. Part of her wanted to run away and pretend none of it had ever happened. But she crossed a line, one from which there was no return.

The life she had known was over, replaced by an uncertain future destined to be shadowed and defined by the consequences of tonight's actions.

She had taken control of her destiny, but at what cost?

# 2

*Fourteen months later*

The bright Miami sun blazed through the office windows of Cliff and Julia Ford's *Undercover Miami Investigation Services*, creating intricate patterns on the polished floor. The room, smartly decorated with matching furniture, felt a bit too big for a business that had yet to secure its first client.

Cliff leaned back in his brand-new office chair and stared at the ceiling fan as it lazily spun overhead. His wife, Julia, sat across the room from him at an uncluttered desk, tidy since there were no business papers to occupy the space.

"Maybe we should have gone with a different name," Cliff mused aloud, breaking the silence. "Something a bit more ... mysterious. Or funny. With alliteration. Like Caper Crackers or the Giggling Gumshoes."

Julia rolled her eyes, a gesture his wife directed towards him several times a day. "How long did it take you to come up with those?"

"I thought of them just now," he replied with pride.

"What about the Crazy Clue Solver?" she quipped, with a wide smile so he'd know she was kidding.

"I got it," he said. "Spy Hard? You know, after the movie. Get it?"

"I love our name," Julia said, ignoring the question. "It's our little secret. We solve cases under the covers." She flashed him a sexy smile that sent a wave of desire down his spine.

"What about—"

"The name is perfectly fine," Julia interrupted, narrowing her eyes. "We need to get the word out. Miami's a big city. Someone will come to us eventually."

Cliff adjusted his tie, which he always wore loosely these days. "It's been a month, Julia. No clients, no leads. I'm starting to think we should've stayed in Chicago."

He expected another eye roll, but it didn't come.

"Give it time."

"It's so hot outside. We're inside, and I'm still sweating like a pig."

"It's hot in Chicago in the summertime too."

"Not like this."

"You'll be singing a different tune in January when it's three below zero in Chicago and seventy-eight degrees here."

"I'll give you that."

"This is where God wants us, honey. My parents are here, and they love spending time with Rita. She needs to be close to her grandparents."

Their daughter would start first grade in August and Cliff knew they couldn't uproot her again. Going back to Chicago wasn't an option, but it still felt good to vent.

"I haven't been shot at in several months," he declared. "I miss it."

She twisted her lips to the side in disapproval. "Most *sane* people don't think getting shot at is a good thing. I, for one, am glad you're not in constant danger anymore. I'm sleeping a lot better in Miami than I did in Chicago."

Cliff was sleeping better as well. His stress level had plummeted significantly. That's one of the reasons they moved to Miami and started a private investigation company. It had some level of excitement but with a lot less risk.

He rubbed his hands together in quick motions. "I can't stand sitting behind a desk all day. I need some action."

"I'll give you some action," Julie said, flashing another playful smirk.

"That's not the kind of action I'm talking about. Although I wouldn't mind it. You know we haven't properly christened the offices. I could close the blinds."

"What about Lieutenant Duffy?" Julia asked, ignoring the advance. "Have you talked to him lately?"

Cliff shook his head. "I met with him once and followed up with a call. I don't want to bother him."

Lieutenant Duffy was the head of the homicide division in that section of Miami. Cliff thought connecting with local law enforcement would help him get some business. Police departments often hired private investigators to work on cases. Since Cliff was a decorated homicide detective with years of experience, the Lieutenant was receptive and assured him he'd send them some business.

Duffy had even offered him a job on the spot, but Cliff politely declined. He didn't mention it to Julia, knowing she'd be adamantly opposed to it. He agreed with her and would only consider it as a last resort.

Julia was right. The business would eventually take off. Like she said, these things take time. Patience wasn't one of Cliff's better qualities.

Julia abruptly stood from her chair, walked over, and sat on his lap. She brushed his hair to the side before resting her arm around his neck.

"We have to give Miami a chance," she said sweetly, kissing him lightly on the lips. "Don't you enjoy working with me better than all those smelly detectives in Chicago?"

He could smell the lavender from her shampoo.

"It definitely has its advantages," he said, returning her kiss with more passion, which she reciprocated in her Cuban way.

Julia was born in Miami to Cuban parents, and it showed in everything she did. She was the most passionate person he had ever met. In everything. Work and in their personal life.

"I'm ready to get to work on a case," Cliff said with a frustrated whine.

"Enjoy the vacation while it lasts. You deserve it. You worked hard in Chicago. Thankfully, we have a couple years' cushion to allow you to take some time off."

"But I don't want time off. I need to work. Solving murders is in my blood."

Julia chuckled. "I don't think we'll be getting any murder cases here. I'd settle for catching a few cheaters or finding some missing persons."

Her eyes lit up with an idea. "You should reach out to bail bondsmen. They deal with people who skip bail all the time. I'm sure they could use someone to find them."

He shook his head. "Those companies have their own PIs on staff."

"Oh well. It's a thought."

"And a good one." He didn't want to dissuade her from coming up with more.

Bottom line, he needed to think of a way to get some clients, but he wasn't sure how to do it. As a homicide detective, cases came to him without effort. There was no shortage of murders to investigate in Chicago. It wasn't unusual for twenty to thirty murders to occur over the weekend.

If anything, Cliff had more work than he could handle. The bullpen in the Chicago police station was a constant flurry of sound and activity—a sharp contrast to his current situation.

As Julia opened her mouth to respond, the door to their office swung open with a rush of wind behind it. A petite, elderly woman stepped in filling the room with unexpected energy. She wore a bright purple flowery dress and exuded a vision of eccentricity. Accented by a flamboyant hat with feathers that seemed more appropriate for a royal wedding than a visit to a detective agency.

"Good morning!" she declared, her voice surprisingly strong for her age. "I'm Penelope Plumley, and I have a job for you."

Julia bolted out of his lap. Cliff had to catch himself to keep from falling backward. After he regained his balance, he stood and instinctively tightened his tie, intrigued by the unusual sight standing in front of him.

Julia was next to the woman in a flash, taking her arm and leading her to a chair across from Cliff's desk. The lady immediately sat down with a tired thank you. Cliff sat back down in his chair, and Julia sat on the edge of his desk, leaning forward toward their unexpected visitor.

"What can we do for you, Ms. Plumley?" Julia asked, her voice friendly but professional.

Penelope adjusted her hat, which had begun to slip to one side. "I have a cat named Snowball. Every morning, I let him out at nine a.m. sharp, and he doesn't return until five in the afternoon. I want to know what he's doing all day."

Cliff blinked several times in disbelief. "You want us to follow your cat?"

Penelope's eyes twinkled with amusement. "Yes, that's exactly what I need. I must know what my Snowball is up to. And I'm too old to track him."

Cliff wondered if this was a test of some sort. "I don't know—"

"Do you have a picture of your cat?" Julia asked.

*Was Julia actually considering working with this woman?*

Penelope's eyes lit up as she immediately rummaged through her oversized bag and produced a wallet filled with pictures of her beloved cat.

Julia took the wallet in her hand. "Ooh, he's so handsome." she said, almost purring.

"He's my pride and joy," Penelope beamed.

"Tell us about yourself," Julia prompted while flashing one of the pictures at Cliff. He gave an obligatory look but didn't bother studying it like he might if it were a missing person.

Cliff smiled admiringly at his wife. She was definitely the more outgoing one and better at dealing with customers. He'd focus on the investigations while she handled the rest of the business. That made them a good team. It felt good to finally see it in action, even if this wasn't a real case to pursue.

Penelope began speaking faster. "My late husband was an Admiral in the Navy. He ran the naval base in Key West for thirty years. Did I mention that I live in Key West?"

"No, you didn't," Cliff said roughly. "Are you expecting us to go all the way to Key West to look for your lost cat?" He regretted his tone as soon as the words left his mouth.

Julia glared at him.

"He's not lost," Penelope said. "I know where he is. He's home with me at night. What I want to know is what he does during the day when I'm at work. Did I tell you I own a jewelry store?"

Cliff could've guessed. She was a walking jewelry store.

"Key West is three hours away from here," Cliff said in a softer tone.

"It's forty-six minutes by plane," Penelope countered.

"It'd be expensive for me to fly down there."

"I have money. I'm prepared to pay you $20,000 for this job."

Cliff felt his mouth drop open in shock.

"Ten thousand up front and another ten thousand when you finish the job," she added.

Cliff choked back a laugh. It almost sounded like she meant it. It had to be a joke. He looked around the office for a hidden camera. Was someone trying to spoof him?

"That's quite a generous fee," Julia said, obviously trying to diffuse the tension Cliff was exuding. "Snowball must be a very special cat to you."

He couldn't believe Julia was patronizing this woman. She couldn't be serious. If she was, then she'd lost her mind as well.

"Nobody in their right mind would pay twenty thousand—"

"We will accept your offer," Julia blurted, cutting Cliff off for a second time.

"I like you, dear," Penelope said to Julia. "Him not so much!" She followed the words with a disapproving wave meant for Cliff.

"He's not so bad once you get to know him," Julia said. "I can assure you that he's very good at his job. Trust me, he'll be able to uncover what Snowball is up to in no time."

"So, you believe you can help me?" Mrs. Plumley asked.

"I believe we can."

"Aren't there private investigators in Key West?" Cliff asked. "Surely it'd be cheaper for you to find someone local."

"I've already hired two. They weren't worth two dimes."

"Why did you choose our agency in Miami?" Cliff asked. Something didn't seem right about this picture and his investigative instincts were already flowing and trying to get to the bottom of it.

"I was in town and driving by. I saw your sign. That's why I stopped."

"What are you doing in Miami?" Julia asked, sounding genuinely curious.

"Did I mention that I own a jewelry store in Key West? I've had it for years."

Julia nodded rather than reminding Mrs. Plumley that she had already mentioned it. Cliff was now convinced the woman was losing it.

"I come to Miami once a quarter to purchase jewelry for my store," she stated.

Cliff felt his skepticism solidify. This was not the kind of case he envisioned when they started the agency. "With all due respect, Mrs. Plumley, we're private investigators, not pet sitters."

Julia interjected. "But we can certainly help you. We'll take the case."

"Excellent, my dear." She pulled a checkbook out of her purse. "Who do I make the check out to?"

"Undercover Miami," Julia said, with satisfaction.

The lady put her purse over her shoulder and put the checkbook on Cliff's desk. With a shaky hand, she wrote out the check and handed it to Julia, who examined it.

"There's ten thousand more for you when you finish the job," Mrs. Plumley said.

"I'm sure you'll be pleased with our services."

"I think so. I have a good feeling about you." She gave Cliff a less convincing glance.

"And bill me for your expenses," she said. She handed Julia a card. "My address and phone number are on there. Call me the day before you come so I have time to prepare."

Private investigating might be more lucrative than Cliff first thought. In Chicago, he paid his PIs by the hour.

"I told you to take a plane before. You might want to drive," Mrs. Plumley said. "It's the prettiest drive in the world."

"We will," Julia said. "It's something I've been wanting to do for a long time."

"You'll need a hotel. When you call, I'll tell you where to stay."

"I'm looking forward to it."

"Keep track of your expenses. I'll reimburse you. I'm good for it."

"I'm sure you are."

Julia walked her to the door, and Mrs. Plumley turned and gave Julia a hug. As quickly as she appeared, she was gone. When Julia turned around and walked toward Cliff, she had a determined look on her face.

"Cliff, we need this. We haven't had a single client, and this is easy money."

"Easy money? You want to waste our skills tracking a cat?" Cliff's voice was a harsh whisper even though the woman was gone.

Julia's expression softened, but her eyes were firm. "Cliff, we have to start somewhere. Besides, twenty thousand dollars is a lot of money."

Cliff rubbed his temples, feeling the predicament in his confused head. "Fine. But this is a one-time thing. In the future, let me decide what cases we take. I'm in charge of the investigations."

"That's fine with me."

"We're not turning this business into some pet surveillance service."

"Understood."

Julia sat back down on his lap again. "This'll be fun. Consider it a paid vacation to Key West. My parents can watch Rita."

"We need to make sure the check clears first."

"Did you see the rock on her finger? I bet she has millions of dollars. Her husband was an Admiral for the Navy."

"What if she has heirs? They could sue us. What if they say we're taking advantage of an old lady and her senility?"

"She didn't seem senile to me."

"You don't think it's crazy that she'd pay twenty thousand dollars to follow a cat?"

"No, I don't think it's crazy. Maybe she doesn't have any heirs. Who are we to judge what she does with her money?"

Julia was right. If the check cleared, he'd work the case.

*How hard could it be?*

# 3

Jamie Austen was the foremost CIA assassin in the world. Less than an hour after Mrs. Plumley left, she walked into the offices of *Undercover Miami*. Cliff was so shocked he nearly fell out of his chair. He had to blink a few times to make sure his eyes weren't deceiving him.

Julia's chair flew back as she let out a loud shriek and practically ran to Jamie the second she saw her. She threw her arms around her neck, and they hugged effusively.

Jamie had the kind of presence that demanded attention without any effort, and she didn't need a fancy entrance to make it happen. Framed in the sunlight, her black leggings, white tee shirt, and worn black-leather jacket gave off the typical CIA vibe, like she'd just come from or was heading on a top-secret mission.

Cliff couldn't fathom why she would be walking into his office since they hadn't seen each other in years. Admittedly, his mind was still elsewhere which was why he was slow to process it. He'd been staring at his laptop with a blank page in a file called Cat Case Notes, unable to type a single word as he struggled to formulate a strategy for following a resourceful cat that had managed to elude two private investigators with ample incentive to find out what he was up to.

Cliff stood from his desk and walked over to give Jamie a warm embrace as well.

"Cliff Ford," Jamie said, with a wry smile tugging at the corners of her lips. "It's been a while."

"That's an understatement," Cliff said. "What has it been? Three, four years?"

"Eight years," Julia said, giving Jamie another big squeeze of the neck. "I've missed you, girlfriend."

Jamie wasn't just a friend. The last time they saw her was in Chicago. Cliff was investigating the murder of Julia's sister by a dangerous gang called the Strikers. Not only did Jamie help solve that murder, but she saved Cliff's life and played a crucial role in solving the drive-by murder of his first wife, a crime he thought would never be solved.

"Jamie, what are you doing here?" Cliff asked, gesturing for her to take a seat on the couch in the waiting area.

"I'm looking for you," she replied. "I tried calling you in Chicago, but they said you were no longer working there."

"So, how did you find me?" he couldn't help but ask, even though the answer to his question popped into his mind before it even made it out of his mouth.

"Alex, of course," Jamie said.

"I should've known. Alex probably knows what I had for breakfast this morning."

Jamie's husband Alex was the foremost computer hacker in the world. If somebody needed to be located, Alex could do it in record time. Cliff had forgotten about that valuable connection. It could come in handy someday with his private investigation firm.

Although, that's the kind of phone call he'd only make in an emergency. Alex and Jamie were on the front lines of America's war against terrorism. If she wanted, Jamie could pull out her phone and call the President of the United States. These weren't the types to be bothered by a routine investigation from a local private investigator.

Which was why he had no idea why she'd be looking for him.

"How is Alex?" Julia asked before he got the answer to that question.

"I'm not sure at the moment," Jamie said, with her lips twisted into a smug smile. "He's at home taking care of our twins."

"You have twins!" Julia said. "When did that happen?"

"A couple years ago."

"And Alex is watching them?" Cliff asked, with a slight chuckle meant to exude surprise.

"Yeah. I think Alex would rather be in a shootout with a couple of terrorists than taking care of two kids."

"We have a daughter," Julia said. "Her name is Rita. We named her after my sister."

"I know," Jamie said. "I've been keeping up with the two of you from a distance. Although, I didn't know you retired from the police force and left Chicago."

She looked around the offices. "I like what you've done here," she said. "Private investigator. So, you decided to put up a shingle, Cliff. Isn't that kind of boring compared to what you used to be doing?"

"It beats getting shot at," Cliff said.

"I hear you. After I had the twins, I retired as well. I say retired. I'm still working, just not on the front lines anymore."

Jamie and Alex owned AJAX, an art distribution company that also served as a front for their CIA operations. She had been tasked with running the sex trafficking division of the CIA, rescuing girls from horrendous situations. He wasn't sure what kind of work she was doing now and didn't ask knowing the information was probably classified and she couldn't tell him anyway.

"How's business?" Jamie asked.

"We just got our first client," Julia said, smiling.

Cliff groaned on the inside and felt his face flush with embarrassment as Julia explained what their first client wanted them to do.

As he feared, Jamie burst out laughing. "You're going on a cat hunt? That's too funny."

"She's paying us twenty thousand dollars," Cliff defended.

He wasn't sure why he needed to justify taking the case. But now that they were verbalizing it, the whole thing sounded even more ridiculous than he originally thought.

"I'm sure you didn't come all the way to Miami to see me," Cliff said, smoothly changing the subject.

Jamie leaned forward and her forehead furrowed as her tone turned serious. "Actually, I'm helping a friend, Allison Mansfield. I'm sure you've heard about her situation. It's all over the news. When I found out that you were in Miami, I knew you were the person to help me."

Cliff was caught off guard and felt his eyes widen. "I've heard of her. She's the woman who killed her rich husband. You know her?"

"I know her better than most," Jamie nodded. "I rescued her when she was seventeen from a dangerous situation. She was caught up in something she shouldn't have been involved in. I gave her a second chance. Now she's been arrested for murdering her husband."

"So, she was caught up in sex trafficking," Julia said. "Poor girl. Sounds like she got herself into another bad situation. Was her husband abusing her?"

"I don't know. That's what I want Cliff to find out."

Cliff was ready to interject a question, but Jamie continued. "Early in my CIA career, I went to Belarus because we learned that young women were going missing. We believed they were being sold into sex trafficking. They were. I uncovered an operation where a Turkish oligarch had a mail order bride business used as a front for his criminal activities."

"That's horrible," Julia said.

"They targeted pretty girls at bars and casinos, promising them a wealthy husband in America. Instead, they were taken to Russia and forced into sex slavery. Allison was one of those girls."

As Cliff leaned back in his chair, he felt Jamie's story pressing down on him. He had heard similar stories from her before about girls whose lives she had saved from tragic situations.

"Allison eventually came to America as a real mail order bride through a legitimate organization," Jamie continued. "That's how she met her husband. But something went wrong along the way. I'm not sure what. Her murder trial is coming up soon, and I need you to look into it, Cliff. Something doesn't add up and I can't figure it out. I believe that if anyone can, it's you."

"I don't know about that," Cliff replied skeptically, "She confessed to killing him, Jamie."

Jamie uncrossed her legs, her gaze sharp. "And that's why I'm here. Allison won't talk to me. She won't tell me why she did it. All I know is that she shot Grimes Mansfield and made no effort to hide it. But there's more to this story. There has to be."

Cliff was still unsure. "Jamie, she's rich, and I'm sure she has lawyers who are probably tearing this case apart as we speak. What could I possibly do to help?"

"She does have a lawyer and he's one of the best money can buy. But Allison needs an investigator. Someone like you who knows his way around a murder case."

While the thought of getting back into a murder investigation sent a wave of exhilaration through Cliff's body that he hadn't felt in a while, he honestly didn't see how he could help the woman, even if he wanted to.

"Allison's not some monster who'd kill without reason," Jamie insisted. "She's scared to speak up because she's ashamed. I've seen it a thousand times in the girls I've rescued. I'm certain she was abused by her husband."

"You have to help her," Julia pleaded.

Cliff felt the old familiar tension of a murder investigation rise up inside of him. He had spent his entire career putting away criminals, not trying to find ways to set them free. He had seen too many victims suffer, too much blood spilled. And now Jamie was asking him to take on a case where the suspect had already confessed. It seemed like an open-and-shut case, a prosecutor's dream.

"Even if she was being abused, it doesn't justify killing him," Cliff expressed the argument that had already formed in his mind. "It's not a defense."

"She's being charged with first degree murder. I don't think she should go to prison for the rest of her life," Jamie countered.

"I don't either," Julia said.

"So, you want me to find a loophole?" Cliff asked, his tone edged with frustration and a hint of anger. "What you really want is for me to get her off on a technicality?"

Jamie's eyes softened and her jaw relaxed though her resolve never wavered. "No, Cliff. I want you to find the truth. Allison needs someone who can look at this case without any preconceived notions. And I trust you to do that."

Cliff stared out the window, watching the traffic pass by.

"I don't know, Jamie," Cliff said uneasily. "I'm not sure I'm the right guy for this."

"Cliff, you've dealt with cases before where innocent people confessed, haven't you?" Julia interjected. "What if she really is innocent?"

"I've read all the news reports," Cliff said, trying not to sound argumentative. "Her fingerprints were on the murder weapon. The bullets matched the gun. I'm sure they found gunshot residue on her hands. She confessed on the 911 call."

He paused to let all of that evidence take effect.

"I feel bad for your friend, Jamie. I really do. It sounds like she's had some rough breaks in life, but I don't want you to get your hopes up. She's probably going to jail for the rest of her life, and there's not much anyone can do about it."

Jamie rose from the couch and sat down on the coffee table in front of him. She locked eyes and pleaded, "At least meet with her, Cliff. Look through the file and make sure there's not something that's been missed. If you won't do it for Allison, will you do it for me?"

He wanted to say no. To walk away. But something in Jamie's voice, the way she spoke about Allison, tugged at him. He'd always been good at seeing the truth buried beneath the surface. Maybe there was something there, something no one else was seeing.

And how could he say no? After all, Jamie had saved his life, and he owed her.

"Okay. I'll do it for you, but I'm going to tell you the truth. If she's guilty, I won't try to find a way to get her off."

"I don't expect you to. And Allison has money. She'll pay you whatever your fee is."

"It's not about the money."

"I'll give you a fifty-thousand-dollar retainer. Does that sound fair?"

Julia gasped in surprise.

Before Cliff could respond, Jamie pulled out her phone and declared, "Give me wiring instructions and the money will be in your account today."

"As I said, I didn't become a private investigator for the money."

"I know. That's why I came to you, Cliff. You do what's right, no matter what. Hear her story, take fifty grand, and go from there. You can keep the entire retainer regardless of how much time it takes. It might even be easier than finding that cat."

Cliff chuckled half-heartedly, even though he wasn't amused at the cat reminder.

Julie let out an approving squeal and squeezed his arm in appreciation. "It'll be good for you, honey. It'll get your investigative juices flowing again."

Jamie and Julia exchanged smiles.

Cliff bristled inside and felt the resolve hardening inside him. This wasn't what he was expecting when he left Chicago. Chasing cats and helping murderers.

But he wouldn't turn his back on Jamie and Julia who clearly wanted him to do this. He'd take this one step at a time. He'd meet Allison Mansfield, look her in the eye, and see if there was anything in her story that deserved his attention.

And Julia was right about one thing. He was actually looking forward to poring over the evidence and getting his nose back in a murder book. According to Jamie, he wouldn't have to compromise his principles and could follow the evidence wherever it led.

A memory flashed into his mind. From back in the day when he questioned defense lawyers who represented the worst of the worst.

"How do you sleep at night?" he had asked more than one of them.

"I'm trying to make sure my client gets a fair trial and that you did everything by the book."

Was he now one of those people?

It suddenly made more sense to him. He could help Allison in that way. Make sure she got a fair trial, and that the investigator didn't cut any corners.

Jamie leaned forward and gave him an affirming hug. "I appreciate this, Cliff. More than you know."

"Don't expect a miracle," Cliff said, his tone dry.

She laughed softly. "It's never that simple, is it?"

"Where are you staying, Jamie?" Julia asked, lightening the mood.

"At a hotel."

"Why don't you stay with us? We have a spare bedroom."

"I don't want to intrude."

Julia waved her hand dismissively. "Don't be silly. I want you to. We can get caught up on things. You can meet Rita."

Cliff sat back in his chair, staring at the ceiling barely hearing the conversation. This was what he didn't want to happen when he left Chicago. To build a practice defending murderers.

But there was no turning back now. He would try to find out what really happened that night. Not for Allison. Not even for Jamie. For the truth. One thing he learned in Chicago was that the line between guilt and innocence wasn't always as black and white as he wanted it to be.

This was a stark reminder of why he left Chicago. Sometimes the truth didn't matter. Not in courtrooms. Not in a world where people could spin lies so intricately that they became fact.

And now, Jamie wanted him to dive into that web of deception again only this time on what he had always considered the dark side.

# 4

Cliff Ford had seen his share of crime scenes but wasn't prepared for the feeling that overcame him when they arrived at the mansion where Grimes Mansfield had met his end. It felt weird to go there as a member of the defense team.

Allison's attorney, Ty Silver, had reluctantly agreed to the visit, clearly uneasy because Allison herself was so obviously terrified to go back there. But Cliff had insisted. He needed to see the place where it all happened, to absorb the atmosphere and potentially discover something that the official reports had missed.

He hadn't yet reviewed the file and discovery materials provided by the prosecutor because he wanted to follow his usual routine. Normally in a murder case, he would arrive at the crime scene first and then things would unfold in a logical manner.

Earlier that morning, they had met at the sleek high-rise office of Allison's expensive lawyer in downtown Miami. The terrified woman sat across from Cliff, Julia, and Jamie at a massive mahogany conference table, with Ty Silver by her side.

Silver exuded a practiced arrogance that was both obvious and irritating. Cliff used to have contempt for men like Silver but now found himself working for him.

Cliff interrogated Allison relentlessly, grilling her on every detail as if he were the official investigator. He pushed her, while reminding himself not to cross the fine line since she was his client, and he didn't want to risk losing her trust.

Despite his efforts, Allison stuck to her story, the same one she'd given Jamie and the police. She admitted to shooting her husband in their bedroom while he slept, using his own gun. No excuses or explanations, just a stubborn insistence of guilt.

Jamie and Julia both believed she had been abused, and Cliff had his suspicions as well, but Allison remained tight-lipped. This left him with nothing but theories.

He went through a list of possibilities with her, trying to understand what could have driven someone like her to murder her husband.

"Was your husband having an affair?"

"Not that I know of."

"Did you do it for the money?"

She chuckled in a way that expressed anger for the first time. "I don't care about his money. I don't want it."

The district attorney was convinced that Allison killed her husband for his fortune, but Cliff didn't buy it. She already had the benefit of that fortune. She lived in the mansion and drove an expensive car. If anything, killing Grimes cost her all claims to the money.

Jamie reinforced that argument by telling Cliff that Allison came from a bad situation in Belarus and grew up poor which made it even more improbable. Why would she exchange what she had in that mansion for a prison cell? Why would that be more appealing to her? Especially considering that for the first time in her life, she was able to live a life of luxury.

Cliff knew he wasn't qualified to analyze someone's psychological motivations, but he couldn't help feeling there was something deeper at play here. Allison's behavior didn't fit the profile of a cold-hearted gold digger.

No, there was something else going on beneath the surface, something too shameful for her to admit even in private.

When they arrived at the house, Allison emerged from her vehicle, even more visibly nervous. Her hands fidgeted with the hem of her designer blouse, and she kept glancing down the driveway as if, even in death, she expected Grimes to pull in and reclaim his hold over her.

The house was a grand estate in the heart of the city, situated among other extravagant homes with manicured lawns and pristine architecture that oozed wealth and power. Cliff had grown to despise this kind of excessive display of wealth.

How many times had he stood in mansions like this, peeling back layers of deceit spun by the wealthy, only to find they thought their money could erase any consequence of their actions?

But Allison didn't strike him as that type. She wasn't trying to hide or cover up anything. Her behavior didn't make sense.

"This is Grimes's house," she said in a barely audible whisper, leading Cliff and the others toward the front door.

He couldn't help but notice that she didn't say "our house" or "my house." Clearly, she never felt at home there.

Allison unlocked the door and ushered them into a massive foyer that belonged in a magazine spread. But Cliff hardly took notice. His eyes were fixed on Allison, searching for any clues as his training had taught him to do. A killer's true nature often revealed itself through actions and mannerisms when confronted with the crime scene, whether in person or through photographs.

He could see the strain in her eyes, the way they darted around the house as though she was walking into a minefield.

"Follow me," Allison said, almost with resignation as if she wanted to get this over with.

As they ascended the grand staircase to the bedroom where the shooting had occurred, Cliff felt an overwhelming tension and seriousness between them. The silence was so pronounced, all he could hear were their footsteps and anxious breaths.

With determined steps, Allison climbed the stairs and stopped in front of a closed door. She hesitated, her hand trembling. When she mustered the courage to open the door, she stepped back to let everyone else go in and obviously to avoid looking inside.

Cliff entered the room first, taking everything in like he had done countless times before in similar situations. But this time, something was noticeably missing. The body. It felt strange to see the room without it. He closed his eyes for a moment, trying to imprint his first impression in his memory before opening them again and imagining the scene as if it were the night of the incident.

The room appeared untouched, frozen in the state it was left in after the police searched for evidence. The king-sized bed was bare of sheets or a bedspread and a small piece was cut out of the mattress, most likely to collect blood stains for analysis.

Cliff mentally noted to review the crime scene photos taken by the police. He wanted to see the mattress in its original condition before it was tampered with.

Allison was the last one to enter and walked over to stand near the spot where her husband died. She gazed down at the bed as if she could see everything happening all over again in her mind.

Cliff observed her from nearby, noticing every movement and expression on her face. He felt a twinge of guilt that he was making this poor woman relive the worst night of her life.

"What were you thinking right before you shot him?" Cliff asked, hoping her answer might reveal something behind her seemingly cold demeanor.

This question could go either way. Sometimes revisiting the crime scene led murderers to confess their innermost thoughts while others shut down completely.

"I was praying for God's forgiveness," Allison replied in a detached tone, as if she knew it was something she'd never receive.

"He will forgive you, Allison," Julia said. "He already has."

Allison reached out and instinctively clasped hands with Julia who stood beside her, her grip tight and desperate.

Cliff pressed for more information. "Did you consider not shooting him?" he asked.

Allison shook her head, her eyes transfixed on the mattress and her voice cracking as she spoke quietly. "No. I had to," she said. "I couldn't take it anymore."

Cliff stepped closer, taking a more confrontational position. "Couldn't take what anymore? What made you pull the trigger? What did he do to you, Allison?"

Allison looked up at him, but her gaze was distant and unfocused as she replied, "It's my fault. I'm to blame. I told you before. I went into his office and took his gun from the safe. Then I shot him."

She closed herself off again, choking back tears and refusing to reveal any more information. He wanted to reach out and tell her it wasn't her fault, but that wasn't his job. Sympathy wouldn't solve this and wouldn't bring justice. As much as Allison needed comfort, he needed the truth more.

He couldn't let himself get too close. Not yet.

Eventually, her lawyer ended the questioning and Cliff backed off.

Jamie placed a hand on Allison's shoulder in an attempt to comfort her, but she flinched away as if the touch burned her skin.

"You're safe now," Jamie reassured her softly. "You don't have to be afraid anymore."

But Allison didn't look or feel safe at all. Her emotions were raw and right below the surface ready to explode like an erupting volcano. If Cliff had continued interrogating her, he might have been able to push her to break down and confess everything that weighed on her mind, but that wasn't possible now.

"Can we go back downstairs?" Allison pleaded, struggling to get the words out through choked sobs. "I can't stay in this room anymore."

"That's probably a good idea," Cliff agreed. "I'd like to see the office where you got the gun."

They all left the bedroom, leaving behind the heavy, musty air of a crime scene that Cliff was all too familiar with. He trailed behind them, taking one last look around. He wasn't going to find in that room whatever secret Allison kept buried, and he wasn't sure he had what it took to get it out of her.

After seeing the office where she got the gun, Cliff still felt unsatisfied. "I want to see the rest of the house," he stated firmly. "Every room."

Allison stiffened at his words, her eyes darting toward the hallway that led off from the main living area where they were now standing.

"There's nothing else to see," she insisted quickly.

"Why is that necessary?" her lawyer interjected. "I think she's been through enough trauma for one day."

Jamie furrowed her brow, picking up on Allison's sudden change in demeanor. Cliff wondered if Jamie had also noticed Allison looking down the hallway. He was certain she had. Whatever skills of perception he had, Jamie had them on steroids.

"Allison, it's okay," Jamie said. "Cliff needs to see everything. You can trust him."

Allison shook her head, fear right at the surface to the point that she could no longer hide it.

"What's down that hallway that you don't want us to see?" Cliff asked.

Her back was turned to the hallway now, her body visibly shaking, further reinforcing what Cliff already suspected.

"What's down there, Allison?" Jamie asked, gently trying to coax out an answer.

"Nothing!" she insisted, her voice rising in panic. "It's nothing important. Can we just go? Please?"

Rather than waiting for Allison to respond, Cliff walked toward the long, dark hallway leading to a single door at the end. Even though there seemed to be nothing unusual about the hallway itself, Allison's reaction sparked his curiosity, and he had to investigate further.

The hallway was unnaturally quiet, as if the house itself was holding its breath. Cliff's skin prickled as he neared the door. His heart did a somersault when he found it locked.

*What?*

He returned to the main living area and exchanged a look with Jamie.

"The door is locked, Allison," Cliff said. "Why? What's in that room?"

She didn't answer.

"Allison, we need to see it," Jamie said, her tone gentle but firm. "Whatever's behind that door, it's part of this."

Allison's face went white, and she backed away, tears streaming down her cheeks. Cliff watched as she visibly fought some inner battle, her breath coming in short, ragged bursts.

Whatever was behind that door terrified her more than anything else in the house. Even more than the bedroom where she shot him.

"Allison, it's okay," Jamie said, but Allison wasn't listening. She was staring at the wall, frozen in place.

Julia moved closer to Allison, whispering softly. "You don't have to do this alone. We are here with you. He can never hurt you again."

While Cliff appreciated the comforting words from Julia, he knew that wasn't entirely true. Grimes was hurting Allison right now, and he would continue hurting her for the rest of her life if she didn't let go of the secret tormenting her.

For a long and tense moment of hesitation, it seemed like Allison would refuse.

"Do you have the key?" Cliff asked, trying to spur her to respond.

"No!" she said emphatically.

He was prepared to bust the door down if he had to. He'd pay for any damages later, but right now finding out the truth was all that mattered. He knew when he had reached a turning point in an investigation, and this was it.

"I think you're lying to me, Allison," he said.

Silver stepped forward, his voice sharp. "That's enough, Ford. I'm putting a stop to this. You've dragged her through enough already."

Cliff shot a glance at Allison, whose shoulders had hunched defensively, as though bracing for more.

"We're leaving," Silver added, his eyes daring Cliff to challenge him.

"Allison, I can't help you if you don't tell me the truth," Cliff said with a greater sense of urgency, maintaining his focus on Allison and ignoring her attorney.

Abruptly, Allison walked back into the study and opened one of the desk drawers with Cliff following close behind. She produced a key. Her hand shook as she held it up, the metal rattling against the ring.

Cliff reached for it, but she pulled it back. With a shaky breath and faltering steps, she walked out of the office, into the main living area, then down the hall, with Cliff right by her side, the rest of them following at a cautious distance.

Allison inserted the key into the lock, her movements slow and deliberate, as though turning the key was draining her strength.

She looked like a prisoner unlocking her own cell.

Cliff felt a knot tighten in his stomach. The door creaked open. Allison stepped back. She turned her head, refusing to look inside.

She suddenly burst into tears and began sobbing uncontrollably. Julia was next to her in a flash and pulled her close, letting her cry on her shoulder.

To Cliff's surprise, her attorney didn't try to intervene. He was probably as curious as everyone else to know what was hidden in that room.

"Julia, take Allison to the den and wait for us," Cliff said.

"Come with me, sweetheart," Julia said lovingly, while gently leading her away.

Cliff exchanged a quick glance with Jamie, who looked equally unsettled. As soon as Julia and Allison were out of sight, Cliff entered the pitch-black room and flicked on the light.

What he saw was like something out of a nightmare.

# 5

*Later that night*

In Cliff's mind, Allison Mansfield had gone from murderer to victim.

He struggled with a range of emotions, feelings that felt both strange and familiar. He was no stranger to being consumed by a murder investigation. The difference this time was that he was using his skills and energy to prove the innocence of someone who was guilty in the eyes of the law.

Sitting in his favorite chair, Cliff tried to force himself to relax but found it difficult to process the disturbing events of the day. The beverage in his glass was half-forgotten, the liquid inside swirling as he absentmindedly rotated it in his hand.

Across from him, Julia sat on the couch with Jamie, their faces a mixture of exhaustion and disbelief.

"I'm so angry right now, I can't even see straight," Julia said, her voice shaking with fury as they settled in for a private conversation.

They had finally managed to get their daughter Rita to bed but had struggled all evening to enjoy their time with her, with the haunting reality of what they uncovered at Allison's mansion still fresh in everyone's minds.

"If Grimes Mansfield was alive, I'd kill him myself," Jamie said darkly.

Her words dripped with a venomous hatred that mirrored Cliff's own state of mind.

He was usually good at compartmentalizing, but the images of the day kept clawing at him. The modern-day state-of-the-art medieval sex/torture chamber, the instruments of cruelty almost proudly displayed in a large, lighted glass case like trophies.

Above all else, Allison's broken spirit was foremost in his mind.

Julia's voice was thick with emotion and dwarfed by disgust when she said, "Allison told us everything, Cliff. It's much worse than we ever imagined."

After they discovered the room, Cliff and Ty Silver stayed behind to take pictures and capture the evidence while Jamie went to the den to help comfort Allison and try to get her to open up. While he didn't know the specifics, Julia had hinted during the drive home that Allison disclosed most things, but not everything.

Cliff gestured to Julia to tell him now. He needed to hear every detail, even though each word would make his blood boil. Julia shared a look with Jamie before continuing, visibly struggling to remain composed.

"It all started after their honeymoon," she explained, tears threatening to spill over at any moment. "They watched that movie, *Fifty Degrees of Surrender*. Have you heard of it?"

Cliff nodded. "I think there's also a book with that title."

"Yes, that's right. There are now several movies in the series. They were huge box office hits for some reason. I have no idea why. Anyway, Grimes became obsessed with it. Allison found it disturbing, but for Grimes, it was like a revelation."

"It reminded her too much of what she went through in Russia," Jamie said, bitterness lacing her words.

Cliff could only imagine the emotions churning inside Jamie. She had risked her own safety to save Allison from a horrific situation in Russia, only for Allison to end up in a similar nightmare in America where these things weren't supposed to happen so easily.

Julia continued. "Grimes saw himself as this rich, powerful figure, like the character Joe Lamb in the movie who could dominate his wife for his own personal amusement. But this was no fantasy for Grimes. He made it real. He took it way too far."

Cliff clenched his jaw, rage building inside his chest. He'd dealt with abusers before, but this was on another level. The air in the room thickened as Julia continued, her voice quieter now, as though speaking louder was inappropriate, the subject matter too sensitive for anyone to hear.

"When they built that house, that's when it got dark," Julia said. "That's when he constructed that room."

"Allison wasn't a wife," Jamie interrupted, her face hard as stone. "She was his prisoner. He sometimes locked her in there days at a time."

Cliff exhaled slowly, the implications of what he was hearing stirred something violent inside of him. He'd felt it hundreds of times in Chicago when he sought justice for the victims. Too many times, it crossed over into wanting revenge, but he was constrained by the system.

"Sounds like assault to me," Cliff stated coldly. "I think the case could be made that Allison feared for her life. Self-defense might be on the table or stand your ground. Ty Silver will have to figure all that out."

Julia nodded grimly. "He made it clear that if she ever tried to leave or tell anyone, he'd kill her."

"He completely isolated her," Jamie added, her voice tight. "Allison's from Belarus. She has no family here, no friends. He controlled everything—her money, her freedom, even her ability to leave the house. She had no one, Cliff."

Cliff's head throbbed as he tried to process the sheer weight of the abuse Allison had endured. "We can use this information to help her case," was all he could manage to say.

"Will Allison have to testify?" Julia asked.

"She's not ready," Jamie answered for him. "When we spoke to her earlier, she couldn't even make eye contact. She flinched every time we mentioned the trial. I don't think she's strong enough to face a courtroom full of people, especially not the DA."

"It's usually not a good idea to put a defendant on the stand anyway," Cliff said. "The DA will somehow twist it into a consensual relationship. That she was somehow to blame."

Cliff knew all too well how district attorneys approached cases like this. They were trained to be ruthless, often portraying victims as villains. He could already hear their arguments. That Allison was complicit, that she could have left or called the police, that the abuse was mutual. He wasn't sure if Allison could withstand the storm that was coming.

In the past, he'd been the one cheering them on. A wave of guilt washed over him almost to the point that he felt nauseous. He had to bury the thoughts and be ready to fight on the other side of that battle with the same resolve.

"She already thinks she's the one to blame," Jamie said, with exasperation. "I've seen this a thousand times, and it always baffles me. The victims are the ones who feel guilt, shame, and condemnation. The perpetrators don't have any remorse at all."

"That's why Allison wouldn't say anything to anybody," Julia said. "Even to us. She was too ashamed of what happened. We tried to explain to her that it wasn't her fault. I don't think she believed us. She's afraid God won't forgive her."

"That's why we don't want her on the stand," Cliff said. "First of all, I don't want to put her through that trauma. The trial itself will be bad enough. She'll have to listen to all of it ... the accusations, the—"

He knew all too well what was coming and didn't know how to protect her from it.

"If she doesn't testify, how will we get the evidence of the room in?" Jamie asked.

Cliff pointed at himself. "I saw the room," he said. "I can describe it, and I can get the pictures in as evidence. Those pictures will speak volumes, and I'll tell the court what I saw. The jury will be appalled by what they see. The contraptions were laid out like a twisted version of a gym circuit in an upscale fitness center."

Julia spoke through clenched teeth. "Jamie and I took pictures too. Allison has physical scars, Cliff. Do you want to see them?"

He shook his head. "I'll look at them later."

He'd seen many bloody crime scenes in his day but didn't want to subject himself to any more emotional turmoil. Not tonight.

"I can testify to those pictures as well," he said.

"How can you testify?" Jamie asked. "As a witness?"

"No. As an expert. I'm a homicide detective and an investigator for the defense. I can get it all in, even the pictures of her injuries. The prosecutor will object, but the judge will have to let me testify."

"I'm so glad I found you, Cliff," Jamie said, her eyes widened in gratitude. "You're a godsend for Allison."

"I'm happy to do it," he replied earnestly. "I wonder how many other women are going through the same thing. How many more men have turned that disgusting movie into an excuse for torturing their wives or girlfriends?"

"Thousands," Jamie said bitterly. "More than we can count. Twenty-seven million women globally are victims of sex trafficking, and that's probably a low estimate. Domestic abuse statistics are staggering. One in four women in America. And films like this? They normalize it, glamorize it."

Cliff's right hand balled into a fist. "That's obviously why Allison did it. Killing him was the only way out. That's what I'm going to say on the stand."

Julia leaned in, her eyes meeting his. "Does that mean you can keep her from going to jail?"

Cliff took a deep breath. "I'm going to try. It certainly changes things in my mind. Manslaughter might be on the table. But we have to prove that she was acting under extreme duress, that there was no other option but to defend herself."

"We need to keep this from going to trial," Jamie said. "Somebody needs to talk to the DA and get him to reduce the charges or throw them out altogether."

"I doubt the DA will completely dismiss the charges. It's a high-profile case. It's been all over the news."

Jamie's voice was a mix of hope and doubt. "The media needs to hear Allison's side of the story."

Cliff nodded in agreement. "If we can prove that she was mentally and emotionally abused and pushed to her breaking point, we might be able to argue for diminished responsibility. It's not a guarantee, but it could mean the difference between life in prison and a reduced sentence."

A whole range of thoughts were running through his head.

"We could even try for jury nullification. As a homicide detective, I used to hate it when defense attorneys used that tactic. I'm all for it in this case. It's rare, but there's a chance it could work."

"The prosecutor will argue that she could have just left," Jamie interjected. "That she didn't have to kill him. We have to show that she was paralyzed by fear and not thinking clearly. What about temporary insanity?"

Cliff kept his voice steady. "All options are on the table. We'll need a forensic psychologist to testify about the trauma she endured. And those pictures of the chamber will support her story. Without them, the law won't care. If we can't prove immediate danger, it'll be difficult to avoid a harsh sentence."

Jamie leaned back in her chair, clearly frustrated as she let out a loud sigh. "When I'm overseas on a mission, I'm judge, jury, prosecutor, and executioner. I've killed hundreds of men like Grimes and never lost a moment of sleep over it."

"In America, we have this pesky thing called the Constitution and the Bill of Rights."

"The rules over there are whatever I want them to be," Jamie said.

"I would find her innocent if I was on the jury," Julia declared "That's what's fair."

Cliff nodded, but his legal mind was already spinning. "The system isn't concerned with what's fair. It's about what evidence we have and what the judge will allow."

He stood. "You two should get some rest. It's been a long day. I'm going to stay up and go through the police reports and discovery provided by the prosecution. See what they've given us to work with."

Jamie gave him a tired smile, and Julia stood, stretching. "I'm exhausted. Don't stay up too late, honey. You need rest too."

"I won't be able to sleep. This is a chance to review everything while it's quiet."

As the women headed to bed, Cliff's mind raced. He couldn't shake the image of Allison, battered but resilient, surviving in that dungeon for years. She'd been trapped in a nightmare no one knew about until now.

He sat at his desk, surrounded by piles of documents and folders, the soft glow from his lamp creating long shadows in the room. He leaned back in his chair, rubbing his eyes as he prepared to comb through the discovery files given to them by the DA.

This wasn't just a case to win; this was a life to save.

And for the first time in his career, he wasn't sure he was up to the task.

# 6

Cliff worked for a solid four hours poring over the evidence against Allison Mansfield. The work was painstaking, but necessary. Every page, every line, every piece of evidence had to be carefully examined. He was accustomed to the late hours, having done it for years in Chicago.

As the night wore on, exhaustion turned into frustration as Cliff found nothing of use in the evidence. If anything, he was even more impressed by the prosecution's case. It seemed like an open-and-shut conviction.

But something felt off. Maybe wishful thinking on his part, but the evidence against Allison Mansfield seemed too neat and tidy. He couldn't put his finger on what bothered him exactly, but something was missing from the DA's presentation. Rarely did he have a case where everything fit so nicely.

The only thing he noticed was a missing crime scene photo of the mattress, which raised a red flag but wasn't enough to draw any solid conclusions. It could've easily been misplaced or accidentally thrown away. Countless possible explanations would account for its absence.

Also interesting, he only found pictures with close-up shots in the crime scene photos of the chest area where Allison shot her husband. No pictures of Grimes's head or face and none from further away. An angle that would've captured the entire bed and body.

He assumed the lead investigator took them. He couldn't understand why they only focused on the entry wounds instead of taking a broader view.

This raised enough suspicion for him to continue digging, and he decided to start over from square one. The evidence wasn't presented in a way he was used to seeing it. While this wasn't necessarily a cause for concern, it did make it difficult for him to process it in his usual methodical manner. So, he took an hour to reconstruct the case as if he were the lead investigator.

Starting with information about the victim and suspect. Neither had a criminal record. Allison had never even received a parking ticket or had any encounters with the law. Grimes had several juvenile records, but they had all been dismissed along with any speeding tickets. The perks of having wealthy parents.

Next on his list to organize were the victim and witness statements. Obviously, no one witnessed the incident besides Allison. However, the lead detective on the case interviewed Grimes's mother who didn't hold a high opinion of Allison. Not surprising. The feelings were mutual.

Cliff carefully read through Allison's statement, finding it just as straightforward and emotionless as when she gave it to him. Something inside of him made him dig deeper, and he studied her statement carefully until he had practically memorized it. He couldn't put his finger on what exactly bothered him, so he eventually moved on.

When he reached the autopsy report, he scanned through it once more, this time paying closer attention. His finger followed each line of text until he reached the end, searching for even the smallest detail out of place.

An internal alarm went off in his head and his whole body stiffened.

Something was missing. A page from the report.

*How did I not catch that before?*

Only someone well-versed in autopsies would have noticed such a discrepancy. Surely the lead investigator would have caught it as well. Cliff combed through the entire file but found no mention of the missing page in the investigator's notes.

*Strange.*

Now he had two inconsistencies. Not only was the photo of the mattress missing, but also a page from the crucial autopsy report. This couldn't be a coincidence.

The investigator should have all the necessary documents and would have no reason to withhold them from the defense team. If a page was indeed missing, he could simply request a new copy from the coroner.

Allison's attorney hadn't flagged the issue either, which didn't come as a surprise to Cliff, as lawyers often missed small details during investigations like this. Despite trying to brush it off as nothing, Cliff couldn't help but feel suspicious.

Was he overreacting and seeing ghosts where there were none? Or was there truly something significant about these missing pieces?

Massaging his temples to ease the faint headache that had crept up on him after hours of reading, Cliff considered moving on to other aspects of the case. But a nagging feeling persisted, telling him something crucial was slipping through his fingers.

He flipped back a few pages and saw the name Brett Bauer, the lead investigator in charge of this case. Cliff fired up his computer and looked up information on Bauer. He was only thirty-four years old and had been working for less than two years in the force starting in arson before being recently promoted to homicide cases.

That didn't necessarily mean anything. Some officers with only two years of experience were better investigators than those who had been on the force for thirty years.

As an example, Cliff remembered a detective named Gilberto Espino. He retired four years ago after serving on the Chicago police force for twenty-five years. Espino was accused of framing over sixty individuals for murder.

Cliff had known Espino and had no idea he was dirty. Dozens of people claimed to have been beaten into false confessions. Witnesses also stepped forward stating that Espino manipulated their identifications during line-ups, and that he planted or destroyed evidence on many occasions.

Normally, Cliff sided with the cops until proven otherwise. Recently, Cliff read that Espino testified at a hearing and took the fifth. Refusing to testify didn't necessarily mean he was guilty, but it sure looked bad, and Cliff could only draw that conclusion.

One thing Cliff detested nearly as much as a murderer was a corrupt cop.

While reminding himself that detectives could be bad was certainly interesting, it didn't help Cliff with Allison's case. Bauer had no motive to plant evidence, as he had both the murder weapon and a confession from Allison herself. He hadn't coerced her into confessing anything since she essentially told Cliff the same story.

Still, two pieces of evidence were missing with no clear explanation. *Were they missing or destroyed?*

Why would Bauer destroy them? What valuable information could be found on that page in the autopsy report that could aid the defense? And what might the crime scene photos reveal that would contradict Allison's version of events?

Cliff was grasping at thin air, but it's all he had to work with.

The two bullet wounds to the chest were clearly documented and enough to confirm Allison's account of shooting the victim. The coroner's determination of homicide as the cause of death also supported her story.

Still, why leave room for doubt when there was such a strong case against Allison?

A defense attorney would jump at the opportunity to use this against the prosecution in court. An incomplete file was careless at best and suspicious at worst. Allison's attorney, Silver, would surely bring up these issues at trial, questioning the detective's competency and integrity. He was a capable attorney and only needed a small opening to plant seeds of reasonable doubt in the minds of the jury.

If Cliff couldn't understand why the autopsy photo was missing, neither would the twelve members who would decide Allison's fate. He could hear Silver now, asking questions in his folksy manner.

"What are the investigators trying to cover up?"

"What else are they hiding?"

"If they're that incompetent, can we really trust the ballistics report? What about the fingerprints on the gun? Maybe the gun was planted."

Ultimately, none of it would probably matter. These discrepancies weren't enough to sway a jury. He needed more. His job was to find something, and this was all he had. Not much to work with considering how much was at stake.

Jamie suddenly appeared at the door.

Startled, Cliff muttered, "You could've warned me" His heart was racing. "It's a good thing I don't have my gun on me."

Jamie laughed. "Alex and I used to sleep with guns on our nightstands. We started leaving the bathroom light on so we wouldn't accidentally shoot each other. Now with the twins, we can't take the risk."

"Rita's old enough now that I have to keep my gun locked in the safe," Cliff replied.

"Same here," Jamie said. "Anyway, I couldn't sleep. Did you find anything?"

Cliff nodded and handed her the autopsy report.

Jamie glanced over the pages, her brow furrowing. "What am I looking for?"

"There's a missing page," Cliff said.

She scanned the document again. "I'll take your word for it. Allison's lawyer didn't catch this?"

Cliff shook his head. "Nope. But I'm not surprised. He's not a homicide detective. The lead investigator, though, should've noticed and gotten the full report from the coroner."

Jamie tilted her head. "What does it mean?"

"Not sure yet. I need to see what's on that missing page to know for sure."

"So how do we get that?" she asked.

"I'm heading to the station tomorrow to talk to the lead detective, Brett Bauer. There's also a missing crime scene photo, the one I wanted to see the most. The bloody mattress."

Jamie handed the report back. "I'll go with you. Nice catch, Cliff."

"If the detective doesn't have a good explanation, I'll dig deeper."

"I can tell if he's lying. I was trained by the best in the world at detecting deception."

Cliff chuckled. "Good. That's all I've got so far, even if it's not much."

Jamie crossed her arms after setting the autopsy report back on his desk. "What if Bauer is lying?"

"We'll figure that out if we get there. Unfortunately, it'll be hard to prove."

"I have ways of making people talk," she said with a mischievous grin on her face.

Cliff raised an eyebrow. "I bet you do."

"I'm serious," she said, with cold calculation. "Waterboarding is the best method I use. Most people crack after the first round."

"I really hope you're joking," Cliff said, half-laughing.

The look in Jamie's eyes told him she might not be. Her methods had always been unconventional, and he had never questioned them. He remembered Chicago when she single-handedly dismantled an entire human trafficking ring, the kind of thing no local law enforcement agency had been able to do even with all their resources.

"If Bauer's lying, it'll tell us plenty," Cliff said, shifting uncomfortably in his chair, feeling bad about voicing the accusation if only to Jamie. "I doubt he is. Still, I need to know for sure."

Jamie smiled. "That's why I trust you with this. I knew you'd find something."

"Don't get too excited. It could be something or could be nothing."

"I'm prepared for both," she said, her tone steady.

At least Cliff had something to go on now. A glimmer of hope. With only four weeks until the trial, time was ticking away, and Cliff could feel the burden to find something weighing on his shoulders.

He'd feel bad if he failed but would go on with his life. For Allison, it meant survival. Her freedom was at stake.

Cliff wasn't used to thinking this way. He'd always approached his cases like puzzles. Solve them, find the truth, move on. In the past, it's always been about guilt or innocence for him.

But Allison's haunted eyes wouldn't leave his mind. Now that he uncovered why she did it, the lines became blurred. And that terrified him. He'd never been one to do whatever it took to get a conviction and couldn't see himself doing whatever it took to get Allison off.

Still, Allison might be guilty, but didn't deserve to go to jail for the rest of her life.

The image of the torture room flashed in his mind. Followed by the picture of a prison cell. If Cliff didn't find a way to get her off, she'd be trapped again. Only this time with no way out.

# 7

*The next morning*

The police station was a familiar place to Cliff, but today it felt hostile, foreign, unwelcoming. Jamie walked beside him, her expression calm but alert, always assessing. Their intention was to catch Detective Brett Bauer off guard and gauge his reaction when they told him about the missing items in the Allison Mansfield case.

They found him in a crowded cubicle in the bustling bullpen, focused on sorting through paperwork and chewing on a toothpick.

"Excuse me, Detective Bauer?" Cliff said, stopping a few feet away so as not to startle him.

Bauer glanced up, his face initially friendly but then hardened when Cliff told him who he worked for. He barely acknowledged Jamie when Cliff introduced her as Jamie Steele. She never used her real name in public, only with close friends and coworkers. If Bauer tried to find out anything about her on the internet, he wouldn't be able to, even if he knew her real name.

"Is there someplace we can talk privately?" Cliff asked.

Bauer looked around somewhat warily then said, "Follow me."

He led them into an interrogation room that brought back warm feelings, except Cliff was sitting on the opposite side of the table for the first time in his life.

"I used to be a homicide detective in Chicago," Cliff said, hoping to establish a rapport. "For many years."

Bauer's eyebrow raised as if he were surprised by the revelation, right before his lips twisted into a sneer. "Then what are you doing working for a murderer?" he asked in a voice that didn't even try to hide the noticeable disdain for Cliff.

"Trying to make sure you did your job properly," Cliff responded brusquely, feeling offended by the detective's tone.

He hadn't intended to be combative right from the start, but he couldn't help but dislike Bauer immediately. The man seemed to have a chip on his shoulder, and Cliff had encountered this type of arrogance many times in his career. In his opinion, officers of the law were supposed to serve the public and shouldn't act as if they were above being held accountable by those they served.

"I don't appreciate you coming in here and making accusations," Bauer stated.

It seemed like a strange response considering Cliff hadn't made any accusations yet.

Cliff brushed it off because he understood that homicide detectives were a rare breed. It took a particular kind of personality to handle gruesome crime scenes repeatedly and deal with the stress and danger involved in tracking down murderers. That's why Cliff always tried to get along with them when possible, fully aware of the challenges they faced.

He looked over at Jamie who rolled her eyes slightly. Enough for Cliff to sense her irritation as well.

"Now, why exactly are you wasting my time?" Bauer asked.

Cliff bristled.

How quickly he had transitioned to the other side and was now in an adversarial relationship with the fraternity he was once entrenched in. Normally he gave cops the benefit of the doubt, but now, he questioned everything and was put off by Bauer's behavior.

He wondered how many times he left the same impression with suspects, victims, and attorneys, when he was the one investigating them. Probably more than he cared to admit. His natural personality was aloof.

In the last couple of years of his tenure, he made a conscious effort not to let that callous exterior get out of control. Julia helped keep him grounded, and looking back on it now, he probably did get out in time, before causing permanent damage to his emotions.

This visit was good for him. It reminded him of why he left the force to begin with.

"Tell me what you want," Bauer demanded, roughly, when Cliff didn't answer right away. "I could be out solving murders instead of babysitting you."

Cliff didn't take the bait and instead opened the file in front of him. Bauer eyed it nervously, suddenly on edge when he must've recognized the autopsy report at the top of the file.

Jamie stood off to the side in the corner, hovering over the two of them. The scene reminded Cliff of how he used to interrogate suspects. He often had a fellow detective stand in the corner as a means of intimidation.

"I was reviewing the discovery files," Cliff began calmly. He slid the report across the desk. "And I noticed a page is missing from the autopsy report."

Bauer's face twitched, a split-second reaction that Cliff caught. Bauer's jaw tightened, but he leaned back in his chair, refusing to look at the paper. "That so? Probably a clerical error. Coroner's office screws up all the time."

"Clerical error?" Cliff's tone sharpened. "This isn't some lost form at the DMV. We're talking about a homicide investigation here. This kind of 'clerical error' doesn't just happen. Not when I was on the job."

He couldn't help but stick the jab in there. Truth be known, he wanted Bauer to get riled up. The man's attitude had caused his interrogation juices to flow, and it felt like old times. Like Bauer was the suspect, and he was trying to invoke a confession out of him.

"You come in here implying that I'm not doing my job?" Bauer's voice rose, and his fingers drummed on the table. The tension was rising, and Bauer's anger bubbled under the surface. He couldn't hide it on his face or in his mannerisms.

"I'm not implying anything," Cliff said. "I'm only saying that you got an incomplete file here."

Bauer gave a smug laugh. "If you're such a great detective, why did you wash out? Oh, let me guess. I bet you couldn't cut it."

Cliff reminded himself not to get defensive and to stay calm. The last thing he wanted was some kind of confrontation. The prosecution might use it against him in court.

Bauer folded his arms, crunching on his toothpick as he continued to ratchet up the tension. "Listen, Ford. You're supposed to be one of us. Why are you defending some low-rent-gold digger and trying to get her off? She's guilty and she admitted it."

"She's not a gold dig—" He caught himself and reminded himself to take a deep breath. "I'm not trying to get her off," Cliff shot back, his voice edged with frustration. "I'm trying to find the truth. That's supposed to be your job too."

Bauer's face reddened with anger, as he leaned forward and pointed his finger toward Cliff. "The truth is, she killed her husband for his money. Simple as that. And now you're here trying to poke holes in the case. She thinks she can get off because she's got a fancy lawyer, and some washed up detective that's probably charging her a fortune."

Jamie, who had been silently observing, stepped forward and locked eyes with Bauer. "Detective, we're simply asking for the missing page from the autopsy report. I'm confused as to why you have a problem with that?"

Bauer's gaze flickered to Jamie, irritation flashing across his face as he shook his head from side to side.

"And who are you again?" Bauer asked.

"She's a private investigator," Cliff said. "She works for me."

Cliff didn't mind Jamie interjecting herself. He had experience interrogating suspects, but she was a master at it. She went toe to toe with some of the most ruthless and powerful men in the world. Drug lords. Arms dealers. Terrorists.

She mentioned waterboarding again on the drive over.

Bauer sat back in his chair again. Almost retreating. Giving the impression he felt like a wild animal trapped in a tree surrounded by two bloodhounds.

Jamie had a way of bringing out that kind of fear in people without saying a whole lot.

"I don't know why it's missing," Bauer said, trying to act calmer. "And I'll look into it, but I don't have time right now. Unlike some people, I've got real cases to solve." He looked right at Cliff when he said. "I got an important job to do. I ain't no sissified sell out like you two who can't cut it in the real world."

Cliff clenched his jaw. It's all he could do to not slap the smugness off the man's face.

"Did you know that the autopsy page was missing?" Cliff asked accusingly.

Bauer nodded but said, "I didn't know." His voice was defensive. "But like I said, I'll check into it."

Based on the sarcasm in his voice, he had no intention of doing so.

Cliff looked over at Jamie to see if she saw what he saw. Nodding his head while denying knowing about the missing page in the autopsy report was a tell. When body movements were in contradiction to the words, deception was likely.

By the nod of her head, he deduced that she did see it.

"There's also a crime scene photo missing," Cliff added. "The photos of the victim's head."

He produced the photos he had and placed them in front of Bauer. The detective didn't move from his chair. Didn't even look at them.

Another strange reaction. Cliff would've been curious or surprised even. If something was missing in a file, he'd want to know about it.

Bauer only seemed bothered by the question, not the fact that the picture was missing. His defensiveness made Cliff think he had something to hide.

"I don't know nothin' about no missing pictures. I didn't take a photo of his head. If you gots a problem, take it up with the DA. Maybe they lost it."

"I do have a problem," Cliff spat out with disgust. "I despise detectives who don't know how to do their jobs properly."

Bauer shot up from his chair, his hands slamming down on the table. "You don't get to come in here and tell me how to do my job, Ford. You ain't in Chicago anymore. This is my town."

Cliff stood, their faces now a breath apart. His heartbeat thudded in his ears, but his voice was calm, steady, resolved. "I didn't come here to tell you how to do your job. I came to make sure you were doing it. And from what I can see, you're not!"

For a moment, the air between them felt explosive. Bauer's knuckles were white against the table, and Cliff could see the coiled tension in his shoulders.

Jamie stepped forward, her voice cutting through the standoff. "Detective," she said, her voice cool but commanding, "all we're asking for is the missing page and the missing photo."

She pushed Cliff's shoulder so he'd sit back down.

"It's standard procedure to account for all the evidence," she added. "Is there some reason you don't want us to see it?"

Bauer shot her a glaring look filled with daggers.

"I don't answer to you! What do you even know about investigating a murder?"

Jamie didn't flinch. "We're not leaving here until you explain why both an autopsy page and a crime scene photo are missing from the file."

"And how do you plan on making me explain it?"

Cliff laughed out loud.

Bauer glared at him. "Is that funny to you?"

It actually was. Bauer didn't know he was talking to the foremost CIA assassin in the world, who could make him crawl on the floor and lick her shoe if she wanted.

"Trust me," she said, coldly and with precision, "you don't want me to make you. It doesn't need to come to that. All we want are the missing pieces of evidence, and I think you know what happened to them."

The color drained from Bauer's face for a second before it returned in a flush of anger. "I don't know what you're talking about. I didn't know anything was missing."

"You sure about that?" Cliff sneered, his voice raised louder than it should've been. He leaned closer. "Because that's funny, seeing as how you seemed to have misplaced two critical pieces of evidence. Or did you destroy them? Are you incompetent or crooked? Those are the only two explanations."

Bauer bristled, puffing his chest, as though preparing to lash out in an attack. "I don't have time for this! You want to help a murderer walk free? Go ahead! But don't expect me to stand here and let you accuse me of something I didn't do. I'm not the one on trial. Your client is. And I won't rest until she's behind bars where she belongs."

Cliff's fists clenched at his sides. His instincts screamed at him to press harder, to push Bauer until he cracked. Every tell—his darting eyes, the defensiveness in his tone, his tense body language—told Cliff he was hiding something. But Cliff also knew if he pushed too far, the detective might lose control, and this would spiral out of hand fast.

Obviously sensing the danger rising again, Jamie interjected a third time. "Detective, this isn't over. We're going to look into this file ourselves. And I promise you that I won't rest until I find out what you're hiding."

"Are you threatening me? Cause I don't take kindly to threats. I don't take that from anybody, even if you are a pretty girl."

Cliff wanted to tell Bauer that Jamie was trained to kill him a hundred different ways with her bare hands, but he didn't want to do anything to blow her CIA cover. She didn't either, since she was showing considerable restraint.

They did have to be cautious. Bauer had the authority to lock them in jail. Jamie could make one phone call and be out faster than Bauer could eat lunch, but neither of them wanted the hassle or the complications it might mean for Allison.

"I don't waste my time making threats," Jamie said. "But people who lie to me tend not to have long careers."

Bauer's eyes flashed one last look of anger, but he didn't respond with words. Instead, he gritted his teeth and stormed out of the room, slamming the door behind him. The sound reverberated off the walls like a final warning.

"He's lying," Jamie stated.

"No doubt about it."

"I counted at least seven signs of deception."

She waited until they were in the car and outside the station to explain what she saw.

"When someone lies under pressure, their body releases stress hormones like cortisol," she said. "This leads to subtle physical changes. Eye movements, breathing patterns, things that most people can't control. He didn't even realize he was giving himself away."

"We definitely got under his skin. He was sweating heavily and destroyed that toothpick in his mouth."

"Some of the signs were more subtle. His left eye narrowed while his right remained open," she elaborated. "The increased blink rate, rapid breathing, and swallowing hard. He licked his lips nervously. These are all indicators of deception."

"I noticed some of those."

"The biggest tell was when you asked him if he knew the autopsy page was missing. Twice, he nodded as he denied it, while also giving a slight shake of his head, almost imperceptible, but it contradicted his words. He wasn't lying when he said he didn't take a photo of the head."

"I caught that too."

"Now the question is, what can we do about it?"

"There's not much we can do. I don't have the power to make Bauer cooperate. But at least we achieved our goal. I wanted to look him in the eye and see if he was lying."

"And he was."

"But that doesn't necessarily mean anything. All we know for sure is that he knew the autopsy page was missing and lied about it."

"Or they might not be missing. He could be hiding the evidence."

"Right. So let's say he is hiding it. Why would he do that?"

Cliff had no logical explanation to offer.

# 8

*Three weeks later*

As Julia drove them from Miami to Key West on the Overseas Highway, Cliff leaned back in the passenger seat, admiring the sun reflecting off the turquoise water. The road, seemingly endless between sky and sea, should have been a piece of paradise, but Cliff couldn't shake the frustration he felt.

He was accustomed to chasing criminals, solving murders, and facing danger. His current assignment—tracking a wealthy old woman's cat—seemed absurd. The type of case you joked about with colleagues around a water cooler, not taken seriously.

Allison Mansfield's case was on hold until the trial started in a week and Cliff had put off his promise to Mrs. Plumley to find out what her mysterious cat was up to long enough. He didn't mind taking a break from the stress of Allison's case, but this? He felt like a detective who had fallen off the map and was now so desperate to get back in the game that he resorted to tracking down wayward pets for a living.

He hoped Brett Bauer never heard about it. The detective would ridicule him to no end. He bristled inside at the thought of the man he now despised. Part of the purpose of the trip was to get him and Allison's case out of his mind, but it seemed like everything kept drawing him back to the seemingly impossible situation they faced in Miami.

Allison's attorney, Ty Silver, had subpoenaed the coroner's report and got back the same document with a missing page. No one had a good explanation as to why. The District Attorney didn't seem to care and said he gave them all the crime scene photos in discovery, and if there were ever any other photos, he didn't have them.

That meant all Cliff's work had made no difference in the case.

He reminded himself that he wasn't going to talk about or think about Allison Mansfield while he was in Key West, and they weren't even halfway to their destination, and he had already violated that rule at least a dozen times. In Chicago, he often worked on a dozen different murder cases at the same time and knew how to compartmentalize and focus on one at a time.

That's what he needed to do now, but for some reason, he was having a hard time putting Allison's case out of his mind. Probably because he didn't want to be driving to Key West. He wanted to be back in Miami trying to find something, anything to help her.

The trial was approaching faster than a category-five hurricane.

"I still can't believe I'm doing this," he muttered to himself loudly enough for Julia to hear. "A cat, for twenty grand? What's next, finding someone's missing dryer sock?"

Julia smiled without taking her eyes off the road. "You can't fool me. You love the challenge, even if it's not your typical case."

"Challenge?" Cliff scoffed, resting his arm on the door. "I'm going to solve this in ten minutes."

They had rented a convertible and were driving with the top down. An indulgence they wouldn't charge to Mrs. Plumley's bill even though they technically could. They paid for it themselves because they thought the convertible would make it feel more like a vacation.

"We'll all feel pretty foolish if Snowball turns out to be doing nothing more than mooching food off a local merchant," Cliff commented. "Maybe he found some kids to play with every day like the bow-tied feline in *The Cat in the Hat.*"

"Ooh. Rita loves that book. Let's hope Snowball doesn't get us into any trouble like that cat did," Julia replied.

Cliff looked out at the picturesque view, trying to distract himself from the task ahead. Palm trees lined the narrow strips of land between sparkling waters, and islands dotted the horizon like pieces of a puzzle.

But he couldn't fully relax into vacation mode. A part of him couldn't let go of the nagging feeling that there was more to this case than Mrs. Plumley had let on. He had a gut instinct that had kept him alive and out of trouble for years. It warned him when he was getting himself into a sticky situation.

He didn't get it often but had that feeling now. Was the nagging feeling related to Allison or to Mrs. Plumley or both?

What could be dangerous about chasing a cat?

Maybe he was missing something in both cases. As to Mrs. Plumley, it wasn't just the ludicrous nature of their job. Perhaps it was the generous payment, or the unusual sense of urgency in Mrs. Plumley's voice when she hired them. Whatever the reason, Cliff couldn't shake the feeling that this seemingly simple case might be more complicated than he thought.

For a while, he managed to push these thoughts aside when they passed mile marker 118, and Julia cheerfully pointed out that they were now officially in the Keys. She not only drove, but also acted as their tour guide, having memorized every landmark between Miami and Key West.

What should have been a three-hour-and-twenty-minute drive had turned into five hours due to her frequent stops and explanations. She had been counting down the miles to 118 for the last half an hour.

"Thanks for letting me know," Cliff remarked dryly. "I've been waiting with bated breath to get to mile marker 118."

"You pretend not to care, but I know you secretly love it when I educate you on things you don't know. It's a full-time job," Julia teased, winking at him.

He shot her a playful look, truly grateful for her lightheartedness. If Julia was socially awkward and constantly serious like him, they'd have a miserable marriage.

She continued to guide the car along, pointing out various landmarks such as the giant and strange lobster statue along with the *History of Diving*

*Museum*. They made a stop at *Robbie's* restaurant to feed the tarpon, adding more time to their already lengthy drive.

Normally, Cliff would've been annoyed with such a slow pace, but Julia's enthusiasm put him at ease. It's not like they had to be at Key West at any certain time. They didn't meet with Mrs. Plumley until the next morning.

He looked around at the view, savoring the warm breeze blowing through his hair and feeling his tension slowly dissipating. Trying to force himself to relax.

"Look, we're approaching Seven Mile Bridge," Julia exclaimed a little while later.

Cliff knew this meant they were getting closer to Key West, and he couldn't wait to arrive at their hotel. The drive was beautiful, but it's also why he never wanted to go on a cruise. The view of the water looked pretty much the same all the time. Too much repetition and not enough variety.

But he didn't want to ruin Julia's enjoyment and pretended to share her excitement.

"Did you know that Jimmy Buffett got stuck on this exact bridge in 1977? That's when he wrote 'Margaritaville'.

"I wouldn't want to get stuck on this bridge. If you have an accident or break down, what happens?" Cliff asked.

He'd seen the sign to make sure they had enough gas to make the drive. They stopped and filled up for that reason even though they had plenty of gas in the tank at the time.

"I have no idea,' Julia replied with a nervous laugh. "But don't worry, I won't let anything happen."

She was driving because long bridges made her uncomfortable if she was a passenger. Talking about random facts and stories helped distract her from her fears.

"Anyway, while he was stuck on the bridge, Buffett wrote the song sitting on the hood of his car," Julia proudly stated.

"That's pretty impressive," Cliff said sincerely.

Julia glanced over at him and smiled. "You don't look thrilled by my piece of trivia."

"I really am," Cliff replied with a grin he made sure she saw. "I'm not humoring you. It's actually quite interesting."

"Now it's my turn to ask for something entertaining. Tell me one of your cop jokes," Julia challenged with a mischievous glint in her eyes.

"Who's humoring whom now?" Cliff playfully teased her.

"It's 'humoring who.'"

"I'm pretty sure it's 'whom.'"

"Well, I'm definitely sure you're wrong."

He let out a sigh loud enough for her to hear.

"No, seriously. I want to hear one of your clever but corny police jokes." She said it as sarcastically as she could.

Since she insisted, he decided to call her bluff and make her suffer through it. "What's the number one thing you don't want to say when you're pulled over by a cop?"

"What?"

"Did you stop me because of the dead body in the trunk?"

Julia burst out laughing and he almost let out a chuckle.

"Tell me another one."

"Why did the cop arrest the turkey?"

"Why?"

"He suspected fowl play!"

Julia groaned this time.

"You asked for it."

"I'll never do that again."

The conversation meandered as they made their way through the sun-drenched islands, passing seafood shacks and tourists zipping around on rented scooters. They also passed a group of bikers making their way from Fort Lauderdale to Key West according to their sign and Cliff commented that it seemed like a long distance to ride a bike, and he'd never do it.

Julia agreed although she mentioned wanting to rent bikes while they were in Key West. Their hotel rented them.

When they arrived in Key West, the town was bustling with its usual quirky charm: colorful houses, chickens roaming the streets, and artists selling paintings of sunrises and sunsets along the side of the road.

They checked into a luxurious hotel by the water. Something Cliff would never have splurged on except Mrs. Plumley made the reservation and paid for it herself. Their suite had an amazing view of the Gulf and overlooked the swimming pool, with the mid-afternoon sun shining down on its sparkling waves and the dozen or so sunbathers.

Julia opened the sliding doors leading to the balcony and let in a warm breeze.

"I could get used to this," she said, stepping outside and lying down on a lounge chair.

Cliff joined her and tried to relax his muscles. Working a case in a resort town was a new experience. Back in Chicago, his investigations often took him to dangerous and unsavory parts of the city.

He should be grateful that he was in a five-star luxury hotel with his wife, wearing shorts and taking in the breathtaking view. And getting paid more than two months of his Chicago salary to do so. He started to say that he could get used to this but wasn't sure he could.

Even with the view and the constant breeze, eventually his thoughts were consumed by the case once again. It always happened that way in Chicago. He let himself get consumed. Obsessed until the case reached a logical conclusion.

The same familiar angst started with Allison Mansfield and now continued with Snowball. It didn't matter how trivial it seemed. He was determined to solve the case of the mysterious cat. Hopefully, by tomorrow morning.

"So, what do you think Snowball has been up to?" he asked. "Running an underground fish market? Or maybe he's the leader of a cult for stray cats?"

Julia pushed up her sunglasses so they rested on her head and said, "I'm not the detective here. You tell me, Sherlock."

Cliff's grin widened. "I think he's getting some action."

Julia rolled her eyes playfully. "Oh, Cliff!"

"What? You asked for my thoughts. I'm just saying, with his handsome looks and wealth, he probably has a secret girlfriend on the side. Maybe even a few of them."

Julia tried to keep from laughing but couldn't. "Of course. That's exactly where your mind goes. Always to sex. I'm surprised you haven't made a move on me already."

"It's coming."

"I'm sure it is."

"Anyway, it's not impossible. I wouldn't be surprised if Snowball has a whole harem of lady cats. Can you imagine telling Mrs. Plumley that her beloved cat is the Casanova of Key West?"

"You're terrible," she said with a shake of her head but with amusement in her voice. "Anyway, what do you want to do tonight?"

Cliff glanced at his watch. "I want to go over to Mrs. Plumley's house."

"Tonight? We don't meet with her until tomorrow morning."

"According to her, Snowball returns home at five o'clock sharp every day. So, I want to go over there about four-thirty, scope out the area, and see which direction he comes home from. It'll give us an advantage for tomorrow morning."

Julia arched an eyebrow. "A stakeout? For a cat?"

"We're professionals," Cliff replied. "We have to earn our keep. Although, I do feel slightly guilty for taking twenty grand for something that's going to take me ten minutes to solve."

"Slightly guilty?"

"Yeah. She's paying me for my skills. Two other private investigators failed. I intend to show them how it's done."

"That's the spirit."

"Really, the main reason I only feel *slightly* guilty is because it's a small price to pay for the loss of all my dignity."

# 9

The next morning, Cliff and Julia met Mrs. Plumley at her large stately white house in the annex near the U.S. Naval Station. The old woman was as lively as ever, with bright eyes and a wardrobe that seemed ready for a garden party at any moment.

Snowball, her beloved cat, sat on the windowsill, gazing out onto the street with an air of indifference. Cliff wanted to ask the cunning feline how it had managed to evade them the day before.

They had arrived at Mrs. Plumley's house around four-thirty in the afternoon and took their position, hoping to catch Snowball's arrival. They waited for thirty minutes, but by five o'clock they saw no sign of the elusive cat until it appeared on the same windowsill at exactly five minutes after five, staring out at them as if he knew they were watching him all along.

Mrs. Plumley gushed over Julia's appearance while offering Cliff a glass of iced tea.

"I'm so thrilled you're here," she said effusively. Her joy quickly turned into a frown. "That little rascal over there has me stumped, and I'm looking forward to you two solving the mystery."

She gestured toward Snowball, who now sat up and eyed Cliff suspiciously as if he somehow knew they were talking about him.

"May I ask you something?" Cliff inquired. "Did Snowball go outside yesterday?"

"Oh yes, like every other day," Mrs. Plumley replied.

"And did he come back around five o'clock?"

"Just like clockwork."

Cliff raised an eyebrow, realizing his first theory about Snowball's disappearance had been squashed. He had assumed the cat never left the house.

Mrs. Plumley stepped over to the windowsill and picked up the white, fluffy animal that looked like it could be useful for dusting the floor. She invited Cliff and Julia to take a seat on the couch in her living room.

As he sat down, Cliff couldn't help but instinctively scan his surroundings, looking for any clues, even though he didn't know what could possibly be of any help in the investigation.

Mrs. Plumley's house was obviously once a grand estate in Key West, but now it felt like a relic of a bygone era, much like its owner. The high ceilings and crystal chandeliers were still impressive, but the furniture was outdated, and the floral wallpaper had long gone out of style. It seemed more like a museum than a home, filled with antique pieces and old oil paintings, all reminders of Mrs. Plumley's illustrious past with her important husband.

The couch they sat on was probably purchased by Mr. and Mrs. Plumley when they moved in and was covered in plastic, just like Cliff's grandparents' couch used to be when they were alive. The whole place had a musty mediciny smell Cliff often associated with elderly people living alone.

Mrs. Plumley proudly held up Snowball for display, doting on him like a new mother with her baby. Cliff studied the cat closely, as if he were trying to memorize every detail for a police lineup. Snowball's silky white fur gave him an elegant appearance, while his bright emerald-green eyes stood out against his pure coat.

"Snowball is quite special, isn't he?" Mrs. Plumley practically purred as she showered the cat with affection.

"Is he a polydactyl cat?" Julia asked, surprising Cliff.

*What in the world is a polydactyl cat? And how did my wife know to ask about it?*

When Mrs. Plumley nodded in agreement, Cliff was astounded.

His wife had always been full of pleasant surprises. Knowing random Jimmy Buffett trivia was one thing, but recognizing the cat as polydactyl showed a level of intelligence that he knew she possessed but sometimes needed to be reminded of.

"You have a keen eye, young lady." Mrs. Plumley gave Julia a nod of approval.

Cliff could only stare at his wife, who kept her gaze fixed ahead and avoided making eye contact with him. A small smile tugged at the corner of her mouth, indicating she was proud of herself for being one step ahead of him.

Mrs. Plumley lifted Snowball's paw. "Do you see his toes? Six on each front paw, five on each back. It's quite rare, you know."

"You mentioned your husband was an Admiral in the navy," Julia interjected. "I believe they were bred by naval commanders because the extra toes helped them maintain balance on ships."

Cliff would have jumped off the plastic couch in surprise if his feet weren't firmly planted on the ground. How did Julia know all this information? She must have done her research while looking up Key West.

Something a skilled detective would do, which he should have thought of had he not dismissed the assignment as insignificant and unworthy of any preparation.

All Cliff had done was make a lame effort to memorize the layout of the streets, thinking it might come in handy when chasing Snowball through the neighborhood. They'd taken pictures of the surrounding houses and from outside the main gate of the naval station. Mrs. Plumley's house was a stone's throw to the entrance to the station, which made sense being that her husband had been a commander for thirty years.

"This house was built for my husband," the excentric lady said. "After he retired, they allowed us to continue living here. And before he passed away, he made sure I could stay here until I die."

She pointed out her back bay window. "The ocean used to be right there, almost up to the house. But as ships got bigger and couldn't dock in shallow water, they filled all of this in and moved everything so they could dock further out into the deeper ocean. Even then, they had to trench the bottom to make it deeper."

She waved her hand in frustration. "That whole process was a mess. The noise and construction lasted for several years. And when they finished, we lost our ocean view. Oh well, I suppose it had to be done."

Julia complimented Mrs. Plumley's home, and the woman urged them to visit the Little White House nearby. She pointed toward it, but Cliff wasn't sure which direction she was pointing in. He had seen a sign for it but didn't know its significance.

Surprisingly, Julia knew all about it. "Harry Truman's house," Julia said. She looked over at Cliff and smiled.

Cliff could tell she was feeling proud of herself for preparing for this meeting. He felt smaller than a field mouse, like second string with Julia as the lead detective.

"Back in the day, before my husband was named commander, it was the officer's house and served to host important visitors," Mrs. Plumley said. "Did you know Thomas Edison once came to visit?"

Cliff couldn't resist making a joke, "Did the house have light bulbs already installed? Or did Edison come and install them himself?"

Julia gave him an incredulous look.

Mrs. Plumley replied, "I'm not sure." She twisted her lips to the side and frowned, obviously not getting the joke. "But I do know that six presidents also visited there. Eventually, this house became the designated guest house. We hosted many visitors here. Never any presidents though. They stayed over at the Little White House. I did get to meet several of them."

Curiosity piqued, Cliff asked, "So why is it called the Little White House?"

To his surprise, Julia had an answer. "Because Harry Truman spent a lot of time there while he was president. It's where he signed an executive order establishing civil rights in America and where NATO was established. It has been the site of many significant events."

Now she was showing off.

Cliff was preoccupied anyway. Snowball kept staring at him, and he felt uncomfortable. So he changed the subject to the task at hand, "Tell me more about your cat. What should I know about him?"

Mrs. Plumley gushed about Snowball being a true Key West treasure.

"Just like you," Julia chimed in. This brought a smile to Mrs. Plumley's face.

"Did I tell you that Snowball has been on the cover of a magazine?" Mrs. Plumley exclaimed proudly.

Cliff nodded, having spotted the framed magazine cover on a nearby table while scanning the room. He felt satisfied that he'd found something Julia didn't know and had at least contributed that much to the conversation.

Mrs. Plumley went on and on about Snowball's prestigious lineage while Cliff silently categorized him as nothing more than a spoiled house cat. Julia shot him a sideways glance as Mrs. Plumley repeated herself several times before expressing frustration about not knowing what Snowball did all day while she was at work.

"Don't worry, Mrs. Plumley," Julia said reassuringly. "We'll figure out what Snowball has been up to."

Mrs. Plumley took a sip of her iced tea and gave Cliff a knowing wink. "Oh, Mr. Ford, I do hope you can keep up with Snowball's mischief. He's quite the clever cat, you know."

She stroked Snowball's ears as he purred contentedly.

"I believe I am up to the challenge," Cliff replied confidently. "I have successfully tracked down many suspects in my career."

"Don't underestimate my little Snowball. He has outsmarted two previous private eyes who thought they too were up for the challenge," Mrs. Plumley said with a sly grin.

"I assure you, I will not be the one outsmarted," Cliff said firmly. His eyes met Snowball's and he would've sworn the cat was glaring at him. Almost challenging him.

Suddenly, an old cuckoo clock chimed loudly throughout the house. Snowball immediately jumped off Mrs. Plumley's lap. No one said anything for an uncomfortable minute while it finished its job of declaring the time.

"Are you going to just sit there?" Mrs. Plumley finally asked Cliff when the clock stopped.

"I beg your pardon," he replied. "I don't understand what you mean."

"That's his cue," she said.

"What cue?" Cliff asked, feeling confused.

"As soon as that clock strikes, Snowball takes off," Mrs. Plumley explained.

Cliff felt a wave of panic rush over him. He looked around the room but didn't see the white furry creature.

"Where did he go?"

"Oh, for heaven sakes alive. That's what I'm paying *you* for. To find out."

Cliff suddenly realized what she meant. He looked over at the clock again and saw it had indeed struck nine. Mrs. Plumley had said Snowball left every morning right at nine.

"You mean ... he's leaving now?" he asked incredulously.

"You'd better hurry."

Realization dawned on Cliff, and he bolted off the couch, unsure of what to do next as Snowball was nowhere to be seen.

"I thought you had to let him out," he said urgently.

"He has his own door in the kitchen," Mrs. Plumley replied nonchalantly. "He comes and goes as he pleases."

Cliff's heart skipped a beat as he raced to the back of the house where a back door off the kitchen led to the pool area. He groaned as he saw the permanent cat door where Snowball had made his escape.

Without hesitation, he ran outside and into the meticulously maintained backyard. The scent of blooming flowers and gentle swaying palm trees filled the air but did nothing to calm his nerves as he frantically searched for any sign of Snowball.

Nothing. Snowball was gone like a puff of smoke in the wind.

Cliff's heart continued to race as he scanned every corner of the massive yard, darting his gaze back and forth in desperation. With a burst of adrenaline, he rushed to each side of the wooden fence, leaping up to look over but finding only empty spaces mocking him. Frustrated and seething with anger, he stomped around the pool area, unable to believe that Snowball had escaped so quickly.

Like a feline Houdini. Disappearing without a trace.

The realization hit him like a slap upside the head with a two by four. This meant that they would have to wait until tomorrow morning to track him. The entire day was wasted.

He hadn't really considered that possibility. He thought he'd simply follow him to his destination that morning. Simple as that.

"How did he get away so fast?" Cliff muttered, racing around the yard. He was a seasoned private investigator, trained to chase down criminals, not felines. Yet here he was, defeated by a blob of white fur with a tiny brain. The irony wasn't lost on him, and neither was the growing smirk on Julia's face as she watched him from the back door.

Not giving up, he bolted out the back gate and ran up and down the street, looking for any sign of him. Realizing the cat could be anywhere by now.

Embarrassed, he slinked back toward the house to tell Mrs. Plumley and Julia that Snowball was gone. He had just said that a cat wouldn't outsmart him and yet he had.

In his defense, he had been blindsided.

Julia leaned against the door frame of the front door, smiling as he approached. "Guess we'll have to try again tomorrow," she said.

Cliff felt his face flush with anger as he wiped his hands on his pants. "Oh, we will. I'll catch him tomorrow. That cat's not outsmarting me twice."

# 10

Despite the blazing sun and Cliff's earlier disappointment with Snowball, he managed to have a good time with Julia for the rest of the morning. He followed Mrs. Plumley's suggestion, and they went to see the Little White House.

The tour was interesting, but Cliff couldn't fully concentrate as he searched for Snowball among the many cats on the grounds. He scanned every corner and crevice, hoping to catch sight of the sneaky feline.

Julia joked that Snowball might be watching them from some hidden spot. At the time, Cliff found it amusing, but now it gnawed at him.

Could a cat really be that clever? Was Snowball intentionally playing games with him, like a cat teasing a mouse, with him as the mouse? It seemed absurd, but after what happened earlier, maybe it wasn't so far-fetched.

He pushed those thoughts aside as they continued to explore Key Wests famous attractions. They took photos at the Southernmost Point and were delighted by the butterflies landing on Julia's head and hands at the nearby *Butterfly Museum*. Next, they visited mile marker zero and took more pictures before going into a shop on the corner where Julia bought a t-shirt for Rita and a refrigerator magnet for her collection.

For lunch, a local recommended a little restaurant near the harbor that sold delicious Cuban sandwiches. According to Julia, it was one of the best she'd ever tasted. The bread was crispy and fresh and the pork tender and succulent. She liked hers with mustard and pickles. Cliff took off the pickles from his.

After finishing a satisfying lunch, they couldn't resist crossing the street and indulging in a slice of key lime pie from the world-famous *Kermits*. Despite not being a fan of this dessert, Cliff couldn't deny its perfect blend of sweetness and tartness. Plus, he loved that it came topped with whipped cream.

Julia playfully kissed off a bit of cream from the corner of Cliff's mouth as they fed each other bites. It felt like they were still on their honeymoon even though they'd been married for years now. These moments warmed his heart and helped alleviate some of the frustrations that came with solving difficult cases like Allison's and Snowball's.

He couldn't believe those two cases were occupying his thoughts at the same time. The level of importance between them couldn't be more disproportionate, yet the pressure to solve both weighed heavily on him.

"We should have key lime pie every day," Julia said with a contented smile.

Cliff shook his head. "We won't be here after tomorrow morning," he replied, adding another dollop of whipped cream to the side of his lips and pointing for her to kiss it off again.

"Do you really think you'll catch Snowball that quickly?" she asked, ignoring his tease.

He wouldn't answer until she kissed off the remaining bit of whipped cream from his face. She let out a disapproving sigh before obliging, sending another wave of desire through him.

If they hadn't already had a passionate morning rendezvous at the hotel, he might have suggested skipping sightseeing to return to their room instead. But he knew Julia would reject his suggestion and make an offhanded comment about it.

"I'm starting to doubt if catching Snowball will be that easy," she said.

"Have a little faith in me."

"It wasn't so easy this morning."

"I wasn't prepared. No one told me he had a cat door. Now that I know how he escapes, I won't make that mistake again."

"He was pretty fast though. How will you keep up with him?"

"This afternoon, I plan on staking out Mrs. Plumley's backyard and waiting for him to show up. Once I see which direction he comes from, I'll know which way to follow him in the morning. He won't get away this time. I'll be one step ahead of him."

"A step behind, you mean, since you don't know where he's going, and you'll be the follower. Anyway, how do you plan on tracking him? You can't exactly go wandering through people's yards. What if someone calls the police?"

"I'll be careful. Most people will be at work."

"You make it sound so easy."

"It won't be too hard. A piece of cake, or should I say, as simple as key lime pie," he said with a wide grin, wishing there were still whipped cream left for her to lick off his lips like before.

"Maybe," she said. "It's also possible that Snowball is messing with you on this wild goose, or should I say, wild cat chase."

"I'm telling you this cat has met his match. We'll figure out where he goes tomorrow morning and then we can head home. We'll be back in Miami by two o'clock."

"What if you're wrong? What if it takes longer than that?"

"It can't take more than a day. We have to figure it out tomorrow. We have our meeting with Ty Silver in two days to go over my testimony. Allison's trial starts in three days."

"Let's hope you're right. Otherwise, we'll have to come back another time."

"It'll work out. Trust me."

"If we're leaving tomorrow, can we go for our bike ride today then?" she asked.

"As long as we can make it back to Mrs. Plumley's house by four thirty, or maybe quarter to five at the latest."

"We can ride our bikes there."

"Then let's get going."

After returning to their hotel, they rented bikes from the front desk and set out with a map to explore the small, bike-friendly island. Only four miles long and a mile wide, the designated bike paths on most streets made it easy to navigate.

Their 10.3-mile tour began at Front Street and headed toward Truman Waterfront Park. Along the way, they passed by Mrs. Plumley's house and Cliff kept an eye out for Snowball, hoping to catch a glimpse of the elusive bundle of white. It seemed like cats were everywhere, but that could be because Cliff was noticing them for the first time since he had cats on his mind.

As they continued, they rode past famous landmarks such as the Hemingway House and the Lighthouse. They even stopped at the Southernmost Point again where a long line of tourists had formed waiting to take photos.

"Good thing we came when we did," Cliff said to Julia who nodded in agreement.

From there, they rode along perimeter trails with stunning ocean views and made stops at Smathers Beach and Margaritaville Resort Hotel for some lemonade for him and Cuban coffee for her.

Julia took the lead for most of the ride while Cliff enjoyed watching her from behind. Her long jet-black hair danced in the ocean breeze. He momentarily forgot his worries as he lost himself in the island feel and the joy from being with her.

Eventually, they found themselves riding through charming downtown neighborhoods before arriving back at the harbor where they paused to admire the various ships and unique vessels. Julia took some photos, including a video of Cliff pretending to search for Snowball among the boats.

As it got closer to four thirty, they hurried back to Mrs. Plumley's house and made it with only five minutes to spare. Cliff quickly threw his bike down in the driveway and practically ran to the backyard while Julia knocked on the front door to inform Mrs. Plumley of their arrival.

Cliff found a spot in the center of the yard, his back pressed against the fence and his heart pounding with anticipation. His senses were on high alert, scanning every direction like a hawk on the hunt. As the clock hit five on his watch, his body tensed, ready for Snowball to appear and give away one of his secrets.

Julia and Mrs. Plumley watched from the bay window.

Then, like sinister clockwork, the little white cat materialized, sitting on top of the fence, his tail swishing lazily. He had come from the west. Valuable information in Cliff's mind. Tomorrow morning, he knew where to position himself.

Snowball locked eyes with Cliff, and for a moment it felt like they had engaged in a deadly game of chicken. The stare-down lasted only seconds, but to Cliff it felt like several minutes.

Finally, Snowball gracefully leapt down onto the bird fountain and darted into the house, but not before shooting one last menacing glare accompanied by a hissing sound directed at Cliff.

"That cat," Cliff muttered, shaking his head in disbelief. He couldn't help but laugh at the absurdity of it all.

* * *

Cliff woke before sunrise the next day, determined to outsmart Snowball once and for all. He sat on the balcony of his hotel room with a map of the surrounding houses spread out in front of him. He was determined to put an end to this mystery.

It shouldn't be too difficult. The residential area near Mrs. Plumley's house was on a dead-end street with only a handful of houses. Once the cat got out of the neighborhood, the area was wide open, and he should be easy to spot.

They arrived early and Cliff took up his position by the bird fountain, keeping a close eye on the door of Snowball's house. He had snuck into the backyard without being seen, not wanting to alert Snowball of his presence. It seemed a bit extreme, but he didn't want to leave anything to chance.

His plan was simple: confront the cat head-on as soon as he emerged from the cat door. Snowball would have to walk past him, and Cliff intended to follow right behind until they reached their destination.

Julia was also in the backyard, stationed by the gate to keep an eye on the street. They planned to communicate via phone so she could also help track Snowball's movements in case the cat decided to cross the street at any point.

As expected, Snowball appeared through the cat door at nine o'clock sharp. When he saw Cliff standing next to the bird fountain waiting for him, he froze. The two locked eyes in a tense glare-off, neither moving for what felt like forever, each waiting for the other to make a move.

Cliff stood with his arms folded, determined not to back down but stepped a few feet away from the bird fountain so he wouldn't impede Snowball's progress in any way. He held out his hand inviting Snowball to follow his routine.

Suddenly, without warning, Snowball bolted off in the opposite direction.

"Hey!" Cliff shouted, taking off after him.

Cliff's heart raced as he chased after Snowball, the elusive cat darting around the yard with effortless grace. When he thought he had him cornered, Snowball leapt over the fence with ease on the opposite side of the yard, leaving Cliff scrambling from behind.

Cliff hauled himself over the fence and landed with a loud thump on the other side. He looked around, panicked when he didn't see any sign of Snowball.

"Where did you go, you little runt—" Cliff cut himself off, spinning around in frustration.

A sound caught his attention. He turned back toward Mrs. Plumley's house, just in time to hear Julia's excited shout from inside the yard, "Cliff! He's back. He's in the yard!"

Cliff peered over the fence and saw Snowball darting across the yard, his white fur practically glowing in the bright morning light. The cat leapt onto the bird fountain and stopped long enough to look back directly at Cliff as if to say, *nice try*, before disappearing over the fence.

Frustration boiled up inside Cliff and he couldn't help but let out a yell. "How does he keep getting away?" he shouted to Julia, who was trying to stifle her laughter.

"You'd better hurry or you'll lose him again," she taunted, her voice filled with amusement. "I'll take the street."

Cliff was on the move again, determined not to lose Snowball this time. Rather than wasting time climbing the fence, he raced around the back of the fence, hoping to cut the cat off on the other side.

He sprinted into the neighbor's yard.

A woman screamed.

Followed by a rapid series of shouts and commotion.

He looked in the direction of the house and was horrified when a sun-bathing woman shot up from her lounge chair, shouting at him. Frantically waving her arms and pointing at him menacingly.

"Get out of my yard!"

"I'm so sorry!" Cliff yelled, his voice strained with panic as he continued to run in the direction Snowball had gone, afraid the delay had given the cat the chance to get away.

He caught a glimpse of a white flash in the distance—Snowball's escape route. As he feared, he was too late. Snowball had already squeezed his way through a wrought iron fence.

Cliff pushed himself harder, but he knew it was hopeless. He was too far behind. Snowball was too elusive and impossible to catch. Occasionally, he caught what he thought was a glimpse of him, but the white ball of fur was like a ghost. Slowing only long enough for Cliff to get closer, but then disappearing again, weaving effortlessly through fences, bushes, and narrow alleys, leaving Cliff gasping for breath and feeling defeated.

Never leaving the neighborhood. Only running circles around him not that far from his house.

Julia was right. Snowball was playing with him.

Finally giving up, Cliff stumbled out onto the main street where Julia was waiting for him.

"Any sign of him?" he managed to wheeze out.

She shook her head solemnly. "Nothing. He didn't cross the street."

"You wait here."

Cliff didn't want to give up. If he did, it'd be another day wasted.

Frustrated and desperate, he set off once again down the street, scouring every yard and alley for any sign of Snowball. He spent nearly ten minutes looking for the creature.

When he finally realized he had lost him, he went back to find Julia. What he saw caused his shoulders to sag. A police car was parked on the street with an officer standing next to it, speaking with Julia.

The sunbather must have called the police on him.

How was he going to explain this?

# 11

Cliff was still catching his breath when he saw the police car parked at the curb. His heart, already racing from the wild chase, skipped a beat. The sunbather had called the cops on him.

*Perfect.* Of course she had.

Julia stood on the sidewalk, her face a mix of amusement and mild concern as she spoke to the officer. Cliff, meanwhile, tried to compose himself, wiping the sweat off his brow as he hurried toward them.

Suddenly, a car honked, and Cliff jumped, realizing too late that he was walking in the middle of the road. He quickly stepped aside, not wanting to draw more attention to himself. The car passed and he sheepishly waved an apology to the driver.

But then something caught his eye and caused him to freeze in place.

A white cat.

Looking out the window of the passenger side. With a familiar smirk on his face.

His brain froze for a second.

Was that ... Snowball? No, it couldn't be.

But there he was, staring back at him, smug as ever. Cliff blinked, rubbed his eyes, but the cat remained, almost taunting him.

The car continued to the end of the street. For a full second, Cliff stood there, unable to move, his mind refusing to make sense of what just happened.

*How? Who was driving? Where were they going?*

He wanted to chase after the car but thought better of it. The officer might mistake it for fleeing.

As he neared Julia and the officer, he caught the tail end of Julia's explanation. "You see, sir, my husband isn't a criminal or a peeping Tom. He's just, well … chasing a cat."

The officer looked skeptical, his sunglasses hiding his eyes but not the clear disbelief etched into the frown on his lips.

"A cat, huh?" he asked.

Cliff approached cautiously. The officer stiffened.

"Is this man your husband?" he asked her.

"I've never seen that man before in my life," Julia said, with a smile on her face so the officer would know she was kidding.

Cliff was not amused. The officer's expression didn't falter either as he maintained a stoic and intimidating demeanor. A tactic Cliff had used many times before.

Cliff held out his hand and introduced himself with a friendly tone, "Cliff Ford, is my name. I *am* her husband, though I can understand why she might hesitate to admit it right now."

The officer made no move to shake Cliff's hand, keeping it firmly placed on the gun holstered at his hip. Cliff couldn't blame him. He would do the same thing in that situation. Assess the potential threat before letting his guard down.

"This is all a big misunderstanding," Cliff said calmly, even though his heart was doing laps around his chest.

"Would you mind explaining why you were trespassing on private property?" the officer asked in an accusatory tone.

"I wouldn't say I was trespassing," Cliff defended. "More like passing through. Like my wife mentioned, we were … uh, I was chasing after a cat."

"Why were you chasing your cat?"

"Actually, he's not my cat. It's not what it looks like, officer. I'm a private investigator. And a retired homicide detective from Chicago."

His right eyebrow raised in curiosity. Cliff thought the revelation might buy him some goodwill with the officer.

The policeman's fingers still hovered near the gun on his hip, and Cliff's stomach twisted when he began tapping it. One wrong move, and this whole cat-chase mess could turn ugly.

Cliff's mouth was parched as he offered a smile to diffuse the tense situation. He'd seen things spiral out of control before, and he wasn't about to let that happen today.

"Do you mind if I reach in my pocket for my ID?" Cliff asked cautiously, thinking it smart not to make any sudden movements.

He nodded. "Go ahead."

Cliff pulled out his wallet and showed his PI license and badge. The officer glanced at it but didn't ask him to take it out.

"I'm working on a case. Mrs. Plumley hired us to find her cat, Snowball."

He gestured toward Mrs. Plumley's house down the street, hoping the officer would recognize the name. "We were trying to catch him, well, I was. Julia is just here for moral support. She has nothing to do with why you were called."

He didn't want to implicate her just in case. The homeowner might insist on pressing charges. Hopefully, Cliff could convince him that this was all a misunderstanding and a waste of his time. From his experience, the officer would be hesitant to make an arrest and spend the rest of the day filling out paperwork.

At least that's what Cliff hoped. The officer's expression was unreadable.

His lip curled, as if he couldn't decide whether to laugh or arrest Cliff. "So let me get this straight," he said with a hint of sarcasm. "You were chasing after your runaway cat and ended up jumping over the fence and startling a sunbathing woman?"

Cliff winced. "It wasn't intentional, I swear. Snowball is the one that led me through her yard."

Julia must've sensed the officer's patience wearing thin and stepped in with her most charming smile. "You see, officer, it's true. Snowball can be quite mischievous at times. His owner, Mrs. Plumley, is incredibly worried about him. That's why she hired us, uh, my husband to find him."

"That's all well and good, but you can't go trespassing on other people's property to do that. And if you're a former homicide detective like you claim, I think you'd know that even as a private investigator, you're not above the law."

Cliff nodded in agreement, trying his best to sound reasonable. "You're right, officer. I made a mistake. I didn't realize there was someone in the backyard when I ran after Snowball. I thought I could catch him and bring him back safely. But I understand now that I was wrong, and I apologize."

Cliff noticed a small twitch at the corner of the officer's mouth and knew they were finally making progress.

"Did you manage to catch the cat?"

"No, sir. He escaped."

"Why is it so important for you to catch him?"

"I'm sorry, but that information is confidential. As a professional, I cannot reveal why my client has hired me."

Cliff was taking a risk by playing that card, knowing that it could potentially provoke the officer. But in reality, he was trying to protect himself. He didn't want to admit to how ridiculous this situation was or have it on record in case the officer did decide to arrest him.

He'd rather deal with the consequences of jail time and paying a fine than face the mockery that revealing all the details would undoubtedly invoke. He could even see the prosecutor in Allison's trial getting wind of it and bringing it up during his testimony.

"I do have reason to believe that someone, a third party, is involved and is taking the cat somewhere without the owner's permission," Cliff said, against his better judgment. "I saw someone drive away with the cat."

"Are you saying someone kidnapped your cat?"

"Not exactly. It's not really kidnapping since the cat returns home every day. But clearly the lady I saw who was taking the cat for a drive doesn't have permission to take that cat anywhere. So, in a way, I guess she's the one breaking the law."

Julia tilted her head to the side in disbelief. Cliff tried not to make eye contact with her.

"Are you saying you want to file a police report for a stolen cat?"

"Not at this point. I intend to talk to that person and find out what's going on and where she's taking him. If it's something nefarious, then I'll get back in touch with your department."

The officer hesitated and Cliff sensed an opening.

"Listen," Cliff said, trying to sound reasonable. "I didn't mean to cause any trouble. I was just doing my job. I won't make the same mistake of chasing a cat into someone's yard again."

The officer shook his head and relaxed his stance, finally removing his hand from his gun. "Okay, here's the deal. I'll give you a warning this time, but you need to stop trespassing. Another person calls and I might not be so lenient."

Cliff quickly nodded in agreement. "Understood. No more jumping fences. You have my word."

"Have you considered putting a tracking collar on the cat?" the officer suggested.

Cliff mentally kicked himself for not thinking of that. He had never heard of tracking devices for cat collars before. He had thought about getting the cat microchipped, but it seemed like too much work when all he had to do was follow him.

As it turns out, that wasn't as easy as he thought. Spotting Snowball in the car would make things a lot easier. All they had to do was wait for the car to return and then confront the driver.

The officer gave them both a stern look before tipping his hat. "Good luck with your cat."

Julia smiled gratefully at the officer, and Cliff couldn't help feeling relieved. "Thank you, officer," he said sincerely. "I apologize for bothering you."

With one last nod, the officer walked back to his cruiser. Cliff watched him go and let out a sigh of relief as the tension drained from his shoulders. It could have been much worse.

"You got lucky," Julia said, playfully nudging him with her elbow. "I thought for sure you were going to end up in handcuffs. I warned you that someone might call the police."

Cliff shot her a look. "Thanks for the "I told you so'. Really helps my confidence."

"Now, what's this about you seeing Snowball in a car?" Her words dripped with skepticism.

"Did you see it?" Cliff said excitedly. "The car! The one that went by while you were talking to the officer. I swear I saw Snowball sitting in the passenger seat."

Julia twisted her lips to the side, then glanced toward the corner where Cliff was pointing. "You're joking, right?"

Cliff shook his head, his heart pounding. "I'm not joking. I swear it was him. Sitting there, staring out the window like he was enjoying a Sunday drive."

Julia stared at him, her expression a mix of disbelief and amusement. "Cliff, are you sure the sun hasn't gotten to you and you're seeing things?"

"I'm telling you, Julia, that was Snowball!"

"Cliff, why would the cat be in a car?"

Cliff had those same questions.

"I don't know."

"There's no way that's Snowball. What do you think? That he's hitching rides now."

"Maybe. I don't know. But I swear … that was him."

Julia sighed and gave him a playful nudge. "Cliff, if you start seeing Snowball flying through the air, we might need to check you into a mental health facility for an evaluation."

"You don't believe me."

"I believe that you believe you saw him."

"I'll prove it to you. We're going to stake out this road for the rest of the day and wait for the car to return. As soon as it does, I'm going to confront the driver."

She let out a groan. "I was hoping we could see more of Key West. We haven't seen the Hemingway house. Then I want to go to Sloppy Joe's. They have an outdoor live cam. I told my parents we'd call them and surprise Rita."

"It'll have to wait."

"There's also a restaurant I want to try. Blue Heaven. They have the best-looking key lime pie. It's made with meringue. Piled this high. I would think you would like that." She made a gesture showing it about four inches high.

"I'm not leaving this street until that car returns."

"We don't have to be back until five o'clock."

"We don't know that. What if the driver comes back early and we miss her? I'm not taking that chance."

She looked disappointed.

"We'll eat dinner at Blue Heaven. I promise. We'll get you some of that key lime pie."

"I wanted to eat dinner at the Kaya Island Eats and then watch the sunset at Mallory Square."

"Honey! I'm working here."

She held up her hands in surrender. "You're right. We have a job to do. That's more important."

"Let's get the car and we can wait inside of it. This is a dead-end street. That car will have to go past us."

They started walking toward Mrs. Plumley's house. On the way, Cliff's phone buzzed in his pocket. He frowned, glancing at the screen. The caller ID showed an unfamiliar number, but the area code was Miami.

"Hang on a second," Cliff muttered, slowing his pace as he answered the call. "Cliff Ford here."

"Mr. Ford, this is Tony from Prestige Security. We received an alarm trigger from your office about thirty minutes ago."

Cliff's stomach dropped. "An alarm? What kind of alarm?"

"Looks like a break-in. The back door sensor was tripped. We immediately dispatched a patrol unit, and an officer is on the scene now. He's reporting the back door was found open and someone entered the office. We can see the person clearly on the security video, but he's wearing a mask."

Cliff's heart had finally started to settle down. Hearing the words break in and mask, caused it to kick into overdrive again.

"Did they take anything?"

"From what I saw, the intruder broke into the locked file cabinet. He made a beeline for it. It's like he was searching for something and knew where to look."

Cliff's grip tightened on the phone.

"Did he take anything?"

"The officer found an empty file folder on the floor. It had the name Mansfield on it. The intruder is on tape, taking the contents with him. He didn't take anything else."

Cliff's heart almost jumped out of his chest.

"Thank you," Cliff said. "We're out of town now."

"The officer tried to close the back door, but the lock is busted. If you know someone in town, I'd suggest you call them and get that door secured."

"Okay. We'll leave for Miami right away. We'll be there within four hours."

He hung up the phone slowly. The call had snapped him back to reality, adrenaline flooded his system. The cat, the chase, the officer—all of it faded in an instant.

His office. His case. And the name Mansfield. Everything had just changed. The stakes raised back to life and death proportions.

Key West felt like a world away now. They were supposed to be tracking a cat, enjoying bike rides, and eating key lime pie every day.

But Miami was the more pressing issue now.

Snowball had his secrets but so did Allison Mansfield.

# 12

*Four days later*

It had been a few months since Cliff last stepped foot in a courtroom as a prosecution witness. Now, the tables were turned, and he felt uneasy in his new role. He used to be the one building strong cases and presenting evidence, but now he sat in the second row behind the defense table, feeling like an outsider in this world that was once familiar to him.

Two days ago, Allison's attorney, Ty Silver, had exuded success in his flashy high-rise office, with his tailored suit and gold cufflinks. But today, he had purposefully toned down his appearance, opting for a muted suit and a trust-inducing blue tie.

Cliff recognized the tactic. Silver was trying to appear relatable to the jury and gain their trust. The prosecution wanted to paint Allison as a money-hungry killer, while Silver wanted the jury to see her as a victim of abuse from modest beginnings with a humble lawyer who wasn't getting paid millions of dollars of Grimes' money to defend her.

What the jury didn't know was that this entire presentation had been carefully crafted by highly paid consultants. Silver had a team of attorneys working with him as well as a professional jury consultant who orchestrated every aspect of the trial, including Allison's wardrobe choice.

Allison sat at the table wearing a navy-blue dress with white polka dots and black closed-toe shoes. Accessories were kept simple and understated. Stud earrings, a delicate cross necklace, and a thin watch.

The jury selection process took a full day, with eight men and four women selected. Cliff had assumed that women jurors would be Allison's best bet. Silver's charm and clean-cut looks could sway them, and surely women would empathize with an abused wife.

To Cliff's surprise, the consultant preferred men in this case, turning his expectations upside down.

"Men are more chivalrous and protective," she had explained, justifying her decision.

According to her, men were more emotional than women when serving on a jury. Women saw it as their civic duty and would go with strictly the facts. While it may not result in a not-guilty verdict, if the men's heartstrings could be pulled hard enough, they might show leniency toward Allison and find her guilty of a lesser charge like manslaughter.

The consultant's words chilled Cliff to the bone, "This case is going to hinge on your testimony, Cliff. You need to convince the jury that Grimes is the one who should be on trial, not Allison. With your background, you'll come across as credible. Make it seem like self-defense. Remember, you're our main witness. The responsibility falls on your shoulders."

As if there weren't enough pressure on him. He'd been thrust into the center of this high-profile case, and his office had been broken into which made it even more personal to him.

Cliff had a mental list of suspects who might be behind the break in, but it felt useless to speculate. He had no way to investigate it. As a detective, he had power—badges, warrants, the weight of the law behind him. Now, as a private investigator, his hands were tied. No leverage, no muscle, just the bare bone resources a citizen might scrape together.

The courtroom buzzed with excitement, and the trial would begin soon. Julia sat next to Cliff, and Jamie sat next to her, watching the proceedings with the same intense focus she brought to everything she did.

Cliff glanced over at Allison. She looked more pained than ever, her eyes hollow and sunken. She hadn't said much since they discovered the torture room, and Cliff could tell she was barely holding it together. The bruises and scars Jamie had photographed were bad enough, but Cliff knew that the psychological damage went far deeper.

Despite the sympathy her story evoked, Allison had admitted to killing her husband. This fact would weigh heavily with the jury, and all she could hope for was some mercy in her defense as a battered woman.

Allison's attorney had filed several pre-trial motions to exclude some evidence including the autopsy since a page was missing. Silver had argued that the oversight cast doubt on the thoroughness of the investigation and that the missing information could be critical.

But the judge, a strict no-nonsense individual known for running a tight courtroom, denied his request. The trial would proceed with things as they were. Silver couldn't even mention the missing page from the autopsy or the alleged missing crime scene photo since he had no proof of their existence.

Cliff couldn't rid himself of the feeling that he could've done more. He replayed the investigation in his mind, wondering if there was a lead he missed, or a stone left unturned that could have helped Allison's case. The odds were against her, and despite his best efforts, he felt powerless to change the outcome.

The morning started with the typical formalities. The judge outlined the rules; attorneys made opening statements; and jurors observed with varying levels of interest.

The first witness called was Detective Brett Bauer. The same man who had brushed off Cliff's concerns about the missing autopsy page. Cliff watched as he confidently walked to the stand. He dressed in a worn blazer that made him look like a seasoned detective.

Cliff harbored a dislike for Bauer barely below the surface. The man's arrogant attitude grated on him. And worse, Bauer perfectly matched the description of the intruder who had broken into their office. Same build, same mannerisms. The way he kept brushing his nose with his right finger reminded Cliff of the man on the security footage.

He couldn't prove it, but suspicion ate at him. Bauer was hiding something, and Cliff was sure of it. Although, he wasn't sure what he could do with that information. He already knew Bauer was a liar and wouldn't put it past him to break into Cliff's office to see what might be in the file. To make sure there weren't any surprises sprung on them at the trial.

Silver had brought up the break in, but the judge had shot that down as well. Irrelevant. No proof that the prosecution was involved at all.

As the prosecutor asked questions, Bauer was cocky, dismissive, and had the air of someone who believed he was the smartest guy in the room. Cliff had always been told that the jury didn't like that type of attitude from law enforcement, but as much as Cliff disliked him, he had to admit the man knew how to handle himself on the stand and didn't think it'd be of much benefit to Allison.

Bauer's testimony was methodical. He walked the jury through the night of the murder, detailing how he had arrived at the scene, made sure the house was secure, and collected evidence. Cliff listened intently, noting the way Bauer recounted each step with a calm, practiced cadence that left little room for doubt. He had all the right answers, and his confidence would surely transfer to the jury.

Then came the reading of Allison's statement from Bauer's notes, the linchpin of the prosecution's case. Bauer was given a piece of paper and read it in a monotone voice, devoid of any emotion.

"I went into the bedroom. Grimes was asleep. I didn't want to do it, but I couldn't take it anymore. I shot him. Afterward, I touched his neck. I could tell he was dead. His neck felt cold. The gun fell on the floor. I left it there and called 911."

Cliff shifted uncomfortably in his seat. He'd read the statement a dozen times but hearing it out loud made it feel more damning. Simple, direct, and utterly incriminating. The words painted a picture of a calculated act, not a desperate cry for help.

Cliff could sense the jury absorbing every syllable, their expressions hardening.

The prosecution played the 911 call, and the jury listened intently.

Cliff glanced at Allison. She stared down at her hands, her face a mask of shame and regret.

Bauer continued without missing a beat, detailing the plethora of physical evidence: the gun, the matching bullets recovered from the body, the gunshot residue discovered on Allison's hand. Silver tried to object several times, but each time, the judge overruled him.

Everything pointed to a straightforward case of murder. The prosecution didn't need anything else to prove guilt.

A cut-and-dried case, just as Cliff had feared.

When the time came for cross examination, Ty Silver rose slowly, making deliberate movements. He locked eyes with Bauer, holding his gaze and letting the tension build in the courtroom. The jury suddenly paid closer attention.

Finally breaking the silence with a calm tone, Silver addressed Bauer. "Detective Bauer, let's discuss your investigation."

The entire room seemed to hold its breath, waiting for the battle to begin.

Silver made some points against Bauer's testimony. For example, Bauer was unaware of the secret torture room. The prosecution objected to Silver calling it that and the judge instructed him to refer to it as a safe room instead.

As expected, the prosecutor maintained that whatever happened in that room was consensual.

Silver didn't dwell on this point for too long. He preferred to bring it up during Cliff's testimony. That's when he would show the jury photos of Allison's injuries. It might actually work in their favor that the judge made them call it a safe room. For Allison, it wasn't a safe place at all, and Silver would drive that point home repeatedly at the appropriate time.

At one point, Silver went at Bauer hard, pressing him—even suggesting—that the investigation had been sloppy. Bauer was slick, dodging the questions with the skill of a seasoned cop. He denied any wrongdoing, brushing off the fact that he'd only been on the job for two years.

"I'm telling you," Bauer said, his voice rising slightly, "it doesn't take years of experience to solve this case. Everything points to Mrs. Mansfield. She confessed. She pulled the trigger. There's no doubt about it."

"Did you consider any other suspects?"

He admitted he hadn't.

"What's the point? She confessed."

Cliff studied Bauer on the stand, his detective instincts kicking in. The stiff set of his shoulders, the cocky tilt of his chin—Bauer was performing, playing to the jury. His smirk, just a little too self-assured, reminded Cliff of the suspects who thought they'd gotten away with it.

But there was something else. A brief flicker in Bauer's eyes when Silver had walked up to the podium to question him. Doubt? Fear? Cliff couldn't tell, but he logged it. It might matter later.

Cliff clenched his fists when he could see it seeping into the jurors. He hated it, but he knew that air of certainty was winning them over.

After a while, a few of the men seemed disinterested, not even trying to mask their boredom. The four women were more attentive, scribbling notes on their pads, their eyes flicking between Bauer and Silver. Occasionally looking at Allison with disgust when the pictures of the dead body were shown to the jurors a second time.

Cliff understood what the consultant meant by wanting to avoid women jurors.

As Bauer wrapped up his testimony, Cliff found himself lost in thought, running through the evidence in his mind once more. It all fit together too neatly, almost too perfectly, and Cliff's instincts told him there had to be something more. That he was missing something important.

The gnawing sense of failure nagged at him like a bad cold. He replayed the investigation over and over, searching for something—anything—he could have done differently.

Had he missed a crucial lead? Had his own doubts clouded his judgment?

Every time Bauer spoke, it felt like a blow to Cliff's gut, a reminder that despite everything he'd uncovered, Allison was still on trial for her life. And he couldn't shake the feeling that he hadn't done enough to save her.

The prosecution continued to build their case, calling Grimes's mom who painted a grim picture of Allison's marriage. From the moment she took the stand, Cliff could see the venom in her eyes. She spoke with the certainty of someone who never liked Allison. Had pegged her as a gold digger from the start.

Allison sat rigid in her chair, her hands clenched tightly in her lap, knuckles white against her navy dress. Her eyes darted to Ty Silver, then back to the jury, her jaw tightening with each passing second.

When her mother-in-law spoke, Allison's shoulders tensed. The mother was lying. At least exaggerating and Allison's reactions confirmed it.

"She was always asking about the family money," she sneered. "One time she asked me how much Grimes stood to inherit."

Allison shook her head in obvious denial.

The mother's words were smooth, rehearsed, but the malice was unmistakable.

Allison shifted in her seat, becoming more agitated as the lies poured out of the mother's mouth. Cliff didn't believe the mom for a second. The jury might see it as well but were moved when the mother broke down on the stand and sobbed about how much she missed her only son.

"That woman wanted to inherit everything," she said. "That's why she killed my baby."

Silver scored some points in cross examination.

"If what you say is true, why didn't Mrs. Mansfield wait until after you were dead to kill him then?"

"Are you aware that in Florida, people who perpetrate a crime aren't allowed to profit from it?"

"Why would she kill him and then confess to the crime if she wanted his money?"

Silver skillfully looked at the jury when he asked those questions. Of course, the mother had no answers.

She also admitted that she didn't know about the safe room. She insisted that it had to be Allison's idea. Her precious son would never have thought of it on his own. He was a good boy.

Cliff felt the rage building, but there was nothing he could do about it. Grimes was anything but a boy scout. He'd felt this before when people lied on the stand and talked about criminals in glowing terms. All he could do was to trust in the system and hope the jury could see through the ruse.

Silver was doing a good job. The jury liked him. Allison was getting the best defense money could buy, but Cliff couldn't help but think it wouldn't be enough.

The prosecution rested their case after two days, and Cliff could read the jury. They were ready to throw the book at Allison.

"We're losing this," Cliff muttered to Julia and Jamie, his voice thick with frustration. "They've got her pinned. Dead to rights. I don't see a way out of this."

Julia's hand tightened on his arm, her eyes searching his. "We're not done yet, Cliff. We've still got your testimony."

Tomorrow would be his turn. It'd be up to him to change the narrative.

He couldn't remember the last time he was this nervous.

# 13

Cliff sank into his favorite chair, but it offered no comfort tonight. The events of the day caused his chest to tighten like a bad case of bronchitis. Making it hard to catch a full breath. More like a vice tightening around his emotions, each twist pulling him closer to a point of resignation.

He felt like he'd been in a shootout in downtown Chicago, except the other guy was the one with all the bullets in his gun. He couldn't help but feel like Allison's chances of walking free were dwindling before his eyes. The prosecution had hammered her with everything they had, and Bauer's testimony had been a particularly bitter pill to swallow.

Had he been the lead detective in the case working for the prosecution, he'd be on cloud nine right now.

Julia entered the living room, carrying two mugs of hot tea. She passed one to Cliff, her hand lingering on his for a moment as she searched his face for any signs of hope. At least, that's what it seemed like to him, but he didn't have any hope to offer her.

She settled into the chair next to him and took a sip of her hot beverage. His mug sat untouched on the coffee table between them where he'd placed it, steam rising from its surface.

Jamie, on the other hand, was pacing in front of them, downing big gulps of her second energy drink. The jittery tension felt almost out of place in the quiet room, but in a strange way, it fit her perfectly.

When Cliff had expressed his pessimism a few minutes earlier, she had said, "In my mind, a fight isn't over until I win."

"Don't you ever feel like giving up?" he asked. "Like it doesn't matter what you do, you're still going to fail?"

"In my line of work," Jamie said, "giving up usually means death. Failure isn't an option. That's why things always seem to work out for me in the end because they have to."

Cliff wished he could feel the same optimism. He'd always been a realist. With no illusions that a rabbit could be pulled out of thin air and suddenly turn a murder case upside down. This wasn't the movies or an hour-long television show where surprises popped up out of the blue to create a happy ending.

"That's what has made me who I am today," Jamie added.

He admired her resolve, but he wasn't wired that way. He recognized and lived by the rules and facts that boxed him in. Like Jamie had said many times, when she was out in the field, she set the rules.

Fight or die. Kill or be killed.

It didn't work that way in America. He had been in courtrooms before, fought uphill battles and faced long odds. But this time felt different. Allison's freedom wasn't the only thing on the line. It was his credibility, his ability to turn chaos into clarity. And deep down he feared losing control of the one thing he prided himself on. His instincts.

They'd usually been right in the past. The burning dart in his gut kept telling him something about the case was off. The detective. The evidence. Allison's demeanor. Her confession. He had been racking his brain since the day he was brought into the case and still hadn't figured it out.

"Jamie's right, Cliff?" Julia said softly, though the words felt hollow. "Allison is counting on you to be strong. I believe in you."

"I can read juries. It feels like they've already made up their minds. Silver's good, but the evidence is overwhelmingly against Allison."

"Then you have to make them look at the evidence in a different light," Jamie said.

"This isn't the kind of game you win by playing tricks, Jamie. This is about getting the truth out there, and right now, their truth is stronger."

"How does a lawyer sleep?" Jamie inquired.

"What do you mean by that? I'm not sure," Cliff replied, confused as to why she was asking such a question.

"They lie on one side, then lie on the other."

They all chuckled, although he still didn't understand her point.

"That's what they did today. Bauer lied to us. He knew the autopsy page was missing. We know that, but we don't know why. The mother also lied. Allison never made most of those statements."

"I know they did, but they didn't lie about the main fact. She shot and killed her husband."

Jamie shook her head and tightened her jaw with resolve. "When I'm out in the field, I try to think like a terrorist. I get in their minds and attempt to anticipate their next move. Then I use their own tactics against them."

"You want me to lie tomorrow?"

"No, of course not. But I want you to consider why they are being untruthful."

"I have considered it. The mother is lying because she's mourning the loss of her son and can't stand Allison who she deemed unworthy of her *precious* child. Bauer lied about the missing autopsy page because he was too lazy to follow up on it."

"Why did Bauer break into your office?"

Jamie was convinced he was the culprit.

Cliff laughed. "I don't know that he did. But, assuming he did, it could be for various reasons. Perhaps to avoid losing the case. He wanted to make sure we didn't have anything that might surprise them in court."

"Maybe. That's what you need to uncover, Cliff. You have to cast doubt on their entire narrative. Once the jury hears Allison's side, they'll want to find her innocent."

"But they won't be able to because there are laws in place. You can't just kill your husband because you claim self-defense from abuse."

Jamie came to a stop in the middle of her step. "Stop talking like we've already lost," she chided. "If you have that same attitude tomorrow, we will lose. Tomorrow's your chance to punch back. Come out swinging. Turn the momentum in our favor. Give the jury that reason."

"I intend to," he said despondently. Wishing he had more to work with.

She walked over and pulled Cliff out of his chair, causing his heart rate to increase. She started bouncing up and down, rubbing his arms and encouraging him to loosen up.

Then, she pretended to box with him. Lucky for Cliff she was only playing around, otherwise, he would've been knocked out faster than he could blink twice.

"Come on! You can't give up. Show some fight!" Jamie urged. She pushed him on his shoulder. Rather roughly.

Cliff pretended to shadow box, jumping up and down slowly at first and then picking up speed. He acted like he was sparring with an imaginary punching bag, making sure not to come close to hitting Jamie with any of his blows.

He had to admit the burst of adrenaline did make him feel better and more energized.

As he sat back down, he felt winded. He needed to get back into the gym. With two major cases taking up most of his time and attention, he'd neglected his daily workouts.

Julia placed a comforting hand on his thigh though she couldn't hide her concern. "You've turned cases around before," she reminded him gently. "This isn't over."

Cliff nodded but remained silent. Tomorrow would be his chance to shift the narrative and plant seeds of doubt in the jurors' minds.

To steer away from the serious topic, Julia turned to Jamie and changed her tone to something lighter. "Speaking of unsolved mysteries," she said, "we never updated you on what happened with the cat in Key West."

Jamie showed interest. "Oh right! You never filled me in. Did you find that elusive feline?"

Cliff and Julia exchanged a glance. "We found her alright," Cliff shook his head. "But not in the way we expected."

"Turns out," Julia added, "we saw her in the passenger seat of a car. Can you believe it?"

"Wait, wait, wait! So, Snowball has an accomplice?" Jamie exclaimed. "Who is it?"

"We don't know," Cliff replied, setting down his mug. "We only saw her from a distance. The woman driving could have been anyone. We got called back to Miami before we could investigate further."

Jamie wondered aloud. "Where do you think she could be taking him?"

Cliff leaned forward, resting his elbows on his knees. "It could be connected to something bigger. We just don't know yet." He shrugged slightly. "Another mystery waiting for us to solve once we get through this trial. We have a good lead though. All we have to do is find that person and confront her."

"I'd love to be there when you do," Jamie grinned.

The lightheartedness of the conversation briefly lifted the tension, but it soon returned as they were reminded of the trial. Jamie's smile faded as she stretched her arms.

"Anyway, tomorrow's the big day," she said, giving Cliff an encouraging look. "Are you okay? Are you ready for this?"

"As ready as I'll ever be."

"You've got this, Cliff. I believe in you."

Cliff forced a smile, but his mind was still clouded with doubt. "Thanks, Jamie. I'll do my best."

Jamie gave them both a nod before heading down the hallway. "I'm gonna crash. Big day tomorrow. You two should get some rest as well." With that, she disappeared, leaving Cliff and Julia alone in the soft glow of the living room.

"How does she fall asleep after drinking all those energy drinks?" Cliff asked.

"She's used to it," Julia replied. "When she's out in the field, she has to sleep whenever she can get it. So, she's learned how to pass out as soon as her head hits the pillow."

"I imagine most of the time in the field, she doesn't even have a pillow."

A brief silence hung in the air before Julia broke it. "Do you remember what we used to do in Chicago, the night before you testified at a big murder trial?"

Cliff glanced at her and a small smile appeared on his face. "How could I forget?"

Julia's eyes sparkled with desire. "It's our tradition. My way of wishing you luck."

Cliff let out an affirming chuckle, feeling some of his earlier tension dissipate. "Are you asking if I want to get lucky tonight?"

Julia leaned closer with a broad smile on her face. "I'd say you could use all the luck you can get."

Without another word, Cliff stood, his nerves tingling with anticipation. He reached for her hand, and they walked to the bedroom together. The familiar rhythm of their relationship and the understanding that went unsaid brought a sense of calm to Cliff amidst the turmoil in his mind.

He got into bed first, propping himself up on his elbows as Julia went into the bathroom. She returned a few minutes later and climbed into bed beside him. He caught a whiff of his favorite perfume.

As soon as she slipped under the covers, Cliff yelped. "Julia, your feet! Why are they so cold?"

She laughed and playfully pulled her feet away. "It's because of the air conditioning. You know I get cold easily."

"Cold? It's the middle of summer!" Cliff protested, but he was also laughing now, breaking through the tension that had been building all evening.

They shared a kiss, their lips meeting softly before deepening into passion as their bodies drew closer. Cliff pressed his lips against her neck while his hands traced familiar patterns across her skin. Just when their connection started to warm him from within, something clicked in his mind, like a door being flung open to reveal a hidden truth. A thought that had been there all along, struggling to come out.

He pulled away suddenly, his heart racing, but not from desire.

"Cliff?" Julia asked, her brow furrowing. "What's wrong?"

"I'll be back," was all he could manage before bolting out of bed and rushing downstairs to his office, barely stopping to put on some shorts and a t-shirt.

"Cliff?" she called after him. "Are you coming back?"

He didn't answer. He needed to get to Allison's file immediately. Fingers shaking uncontrollably, he found it and opened it up.

He read the police report filled out by Bauer. The same one the detective had read that day in court.

*I went into the bedroom. Grimes was asleep. I shot him. Afterward, I touched his neck. I could tell he was dead. His neck felt cold. The gun fell on the floor. I left it there and called 911.*

Cliff hurriedly found his notes from when he interviewed Allison.

*I'll tell you the same thing I told the policeman that night.*

Her words were etched in his mind. Cliff's pulse quickened as he re-read what she told him. Something was gnawing at the back of his mind, something that hadn't clicked before.

*I touched his neck. It felt cold.*

Cold.

The word rattled in his brain like a key turning in a lock. His breath caught in his throat. His heartbeat was erratic, pounding in his ears as he stared at the words.

Cold. He kept coming back to it.

Something inside him snapped into place, like the final piece of a jigsaw puzzle that had been screaming for his attention for weeks.

He hadn't connected the dots then, but now ... the answer had been sitting right in front of him, waiting for him to stop doubting his own instincts.

"How did I miss this?" he said. The words slipped out with the same intensity he felt on the inside.

Julia appeared at the door.

"Missed what, Cliff?" she asked. "What did you miss?"

Jamie was suddenly there as well standing next to her.

"What's all the commotion about?" she asked.

"Allison didn't kill Grimes," Cliff announced.

"She didn't?" Julia and Jamie said in unison.

"No."

"How do you know?" Julia pressed.

"Because when she shot him, he was already dead!"

# 14

Cliff sat rigidly behind the defense table, his arms crossed as the anticipation in the packed courtroom grew. The uncomfortableness of everyone's stares bore down on him, and the low hum of whispers added to the tension like gas to a revving engine.

It had been over an hour since the lawyers had gone into chambers, leaving Cliff alone with his swirling thoughts. He had been in this position many times before, but this time felt different.

In the past, he had always felt immense pressure when called to testify in a murder trial. A single mistake on the stand could lead to a killer walking free and potentially killing again. But this time, it wasn't just any case. Allison's life was on the line.

As part of the defense team, Cliff was fighting against the prosecution who was determined to make sure a guilty person didn't go free. And now, he finally had something that could turn the entire case around. In just a few minutes, he would reveal a bombshell that would throw everything into chaos.

But first, he needed to be approved as an expert witness, something Silver and prosecutor Charles Reed were likely debating behind closed doors in the judge's chambers.

Prior to last night's discovery, Cliff was set to appear as a private investigator tasked with presenting the evidence of the torture room and Allison's injuries. But after what he uncovered in Allison's statement, Silver wanted him to qualify as an expert so he could provide his opinion on the matter.

The judge could go either way on allowing this, according to Silver.

Finally, the lawyers emerged from chambers, and based on their demeanor, Cliff deduced that the judge had ruled in their favor. Reed was pale as a blank sheet of paper while Silver seemed almost elated as he approached the podium.

Shortly thereafter, the judge took the bench and called back in the jury. Cliff was sworn in and asked to state his name and professional background for the court by Silver in a calm manner.

Cliff took a deep breath before answering, "My name is Cliff Ford, and I recently retired after over twenty years as a homicide detective in Chicago."

"In your time as a homicide detective, you have investigated countless murder scenes, correct?"

"Yes."

"And you have examined the evidence in this case and reached some conclusions?"

"Yes."

"Do you believe that your testimony will aid the judge and jury in understanding the facts of this case?"

"I do."

"Your Honor, at this time, I present this witness as an expert in crime scene investigations."

The prosecutor objected predictably, but the judge promptly overruled it.

"The court finds that Detective Ford is qualified as a crime scene investigator and may testify as an expert witness," he declared. "You may continue with your questioning of the witness, Mr. Silver."

"Thank you, Your Honor."

Cliff's heart thumped in his ears, anticipation building for the moment when he would reveal his conclusions. The courtroom was about to be rocked by his revelations.

Above all, he couldn't wait to see the look on Bauer's face when Cliff questioned his haphazard investigation and flawed conclusions. The smug detective didn't know what was about to hit him between the eyes.

"Detective Ford," Silver began, "as an experienced investigator and expert in crime scene investigations, have you reviewed all the evidence in this case, including Mrs. Mansfield's statement?"

"Yes," Cliff replied, quickly glancing at Allison in the defendant's seat. She looked small and fragile, but he had given her hope that morning by confirming that Grimes's neck was cold when she touched it after shooting him.

"Icy cold," she had said. "It sent shivers down my spine."

"I have thoroughly reviewed all evidence provided by the DA and interviewed Mrs. Mansfield myself," Cliff stated.

Silver paused for effect before continuing, "Based on your expert opinion, what conclusions have you drawn from this case?"

"With a high degree of certainty, I can say that Grimes Mansfield was already dead when Mrs. Mansfield shot him."

The courtroom exploded. The noise hit him like a tidal wave—gasping, shouting, chairs scraping as people turned to each other. The judge pounded his gavel, silencing them with a thunderous admonition. Cliff could still feel their eyes on him, burning with disbelief and shock.

Reed immediately stood. "I object!"

The judge slammed his gavel to restore order.

Once things settled down, Reed said, "Can the witness clarify if he is stating fact or opinion?"

"We are getting to that, Your Honor," Silver calmly replied.

"Overruled. Please continue," the judge declared.

"What evidence supports this conclusion, Detective Ford?" Silver asked.

"Mrs. Mansfield herself stated that after shooting her husband, she touched his neck and found it cold," Cliff replied confidently.

He could see the prosecutor scribbling furiously, ready to challenge him. But Cliff was prepared for everything. He smirked. *Let him try.*

Bauer sat in the back of the courtroom, looking like an aggressive bulldog that had been leashed to a stake in the ground. If it weren't for the restraints, he may have charged at Cliff.

Silver had Cliff read Allison's statement again for the court. The one she had given to Bauer that night. Then he had Cliff read his own notes, which were introduced as evidence confirming the same thing.

In a calm and engaging tone, Silver addressed the jury, trying to include them so they would listen more attentively. "And as an experienced investigator, what does Mrs. Mansfield's statement imply to you?"

"In my experience, a body does not cool down immediately after death," Cliff stated deliberately. "If his neck was cold, it suggests that Grimes Mansfield had passed away long before he was shot."

The jury stirred and shifted in their seats, struggling to process this revelation and understand its implications.

Silver said, "Let me ask again. In your professional opinion, Detective Ford, do you believe that Grimes Mansfield was likely already dead when Mrs. Mansfield fired the shots?"

"I wouldn't even say it's likely," Cliff chose his words carefully. "I firmly believe with certainty that Grimes Mansfield had already expired by the time he was shot by Mrs. Mansfield."

The district attorney jumped up from her seat. "Objection, Your Honor! This is speculation. He can't say anything with certainty based on the evidence presented in this case."

The judge, a seasoned veteran with a graying beard and piercing gaze, peered over his glasses at the DA. "Overruled. Detective Ford's expertise qualifies him to give his opinion on this matter. You will have your chance to cross-examine him."

Little did Reed know that Cliff had more bombshells to reveal.

"Detective Ford, does this conclusion solely rely on Mrs. Mansfield's statement about her husband's cold neck?" Silver asked.

"Not entirely," Cliff responded confidently. "Other evidence in this case supports my belief."

"What other evidence?"

"Blood tells a story," Cliff turned to face the jury, making eye contact with each of them as he had been trained to do. "According to the autopsy report, Mrs. Mansfield shot her husband twice in the chest, and two bullets were found in his body."

He paused for a moment to gather his thoughts before continuing.

"The bedspread and top sheet confirm that evidence. The bullets left holes in both. What was noticeably missing were bloodstains."

"There were bloodstains collected in this case," Silver stated.

"That's true, but they were negligible. If Grimes was lying on his back and was shot in the chest, there would have been significant blood on the top sheet and that blood would've run down to the bottom sheet and onto the mattress. Instead, there was only a trace—too little to match the scenario of a living person being shot."

Silver stepped back, allowing the jury a moment to process the implications. Cliff could tell they were thinking it over, the gears in their minds slowly turning.

"Is there any other evidence that supports your theory?" Silver asked.

"Well, that's part of the problem," Cliff said. "I found that the evidence has been tampered with in some way. The evidence that would've exonerated Mrs. Mansfield is conveniently missing."

The court erupted again. As did the DA, who bolted out of his seat and objected.

The judge motioned for the attorneys to approach. From his vantage point, he could hear them arguing about the admissibility of the missing page in the autopsy report. The judge had no choice but to allow it at this point as relevant and said as much overruling the objection.

Bauer glared at Cliff who avoided making direct eye contact with him.

"You may continue, Detective," Silver said. "What irregularities did you find in the investigation? What evidence is missing?"

Cliff leaned forward, his voice steady but firm. "Part of the autopsy report is missing. A single page, crucial to understanding what really happened that night "

Silver put the autopsy report on the screen and Cliff explained how he knew it was missing. Silver put up a normal autopsy report to prove Cliff was accurate and should've had another page attached.

"That page may very well show other potential causes of death along with the time of death," Cliff added.

Silver asked a few more questions, then moved on so as not to belabor the point which had certainly been made.

"Did you find any other irregularities?" Silver asked.

"Yes. I found it extremely troubling that the only pictures of the crime scene were of the shots to the chest. If I had been the investigator, I would've taken pictures from every angle."

"Objection."

"Overruled."

"You may continue, Detective."

"I would have taken photos of the entire body, including the head area. I also would have documented the state of the mattress after the body was moved, but before forensics began their work."

Cliff turned to Bauer, who was squirming uncomfortably in his seat. If looks could kill, Cliff would have been dead ten times over.

"Did you ask Detective Bauer about the missing photos?"

"I did."

"What was his response?"

"Objection."

"Overruled."

"He was being evasive. I believe he did take pictures of the entire crime scene and knows what happened to that missing autopsy page."

"Objection!"

"Sustained. The last sentence will be stricken from the record."

Silver wasted no time in resuming his questioning. His speed added to the dramatic effect. "Because there is a missing autopsy page and lack of photos of the entire crime scene, it is impossible for us to know the full truth, isn't that right?"

"Objection."

"Withdrawn."

Cliff wasn't allowed to answer, but it didn't matter. The damage had already been done. A few of the jurors were now paying closer attention to Bauer, who looked uneasy under their scrutiny.

Could this create reasonable doubt? Only time would tell. The next line of questioning would be crucial. Jamie had urged Cliff to give the jury a reason to find Allison not guilty even if they were unsure about Grimes being dead.

Cliff felt a knot form in his stomach as Silver asked his next set of questions.

"You were the one who discovered the safe room, correct, Detective Ford?"

"Yes, although for Mrs. Mansfield, that room was anything but safe. It was more like a living nightmare."

"How would you describe the room?"

Cliff's chest tightened as memories flooded back. As dark a crime scene as he had ever encountered.

"I'd describe it as a torture chamber. Mrs. Mansfield was essentially a hostage in that room. Grimes would keep her locked up for days on end, sometimes without food or water. He punished her endlessly."

Cliff went on to explain how Grimes had gotten the idea for the room from a movie, and several jurors nodded as if they were familiar with it. Cliff despised that movie and wondered if Grimes would've ever come up with the idea without that movie as his inspiration. It wouldn't be the first time Hollywood had inspired criminal minds to act.

"Detective Bauer said that what happened in that room was consensual. Pleasureful for Mrs. Mansfield."

Cliff scoffed. "That's ridiculous. Mrs. Mansfield suffered severe physical injuries in that room."

"I hate to ask this question, but can you describe those for the jury?"

Cliff hesitated for a moment, wanting the jury to feel the weight of what had happened. Allison looked directly at him.

Her tear-filled eyes met his, searching, pleading—begging for validation, for someone to understand her shattered existence.

He described it in excruciating detail. His voice broke as he added, "I found bloodstains on the mattress in the torture room. Old ones, from previous injuries. It was clear that this had been going on for a long time."

Silver presented the photos of Allison's back as evidence. The defense put up a lame objection but were quickly struck down.

The courtroom was filled with a heavy silence that seemed to suffocate everyone inside. Cliff could see the shock and horror on the jurors' faces as the pictures were put up on the screen. Even the judge looked uneasy in his seat.

Allison refused to look at them.

A murmur spread through the room, a wave of disbelief. Cliff swallowed hard, his throat tightening at the thought of what Allison had endured. He didn't want to look at her, but his eyes were drawn to her trembling figure, hunched over with silent but noticeable sobs.

She seemed to be trying to hide from it all, burying her head in her hands as if to escape the truth of her past. Cliff's heart ached for her, because of the pain she had endured.

It strengthened his resolve even further.

Taking a deep breath, Cliff knew that his next words would make or break everything. He turned to face the jury, his voice hoarse but steady.

"Grimes Mansfield didn't just kill her spirit—he trapped her in a prison so dark, she couldn't see any other way out. When she pulled that trigger, she wasn't just saving herself from him. She was saving what little was left of her humanity."

"As a crime scene investigator, would you consider her actions self-defense?" Silver asked.

"In a way, yes. Allison didn't have a choice anymore. That room wasn't just a place of punishment, it was a place of death. She was afraid that he'd eventually kill her which he had threatened to do many times. In a way, he already had. He had killed all her hopes and dreams for a good life. She came to America in pursuit of a life of freedom. That was no longer an option for her. She saw killing him as her only way out. She preferred the prison the state would send her to over the prison she was already in. That's why she shot him."

"But Grimes was already dead? In your opinion, she didn't murder him, did she?"

"No. He died in that room long before she pulled the trigger. His neck was cold."

If a penny dropped in the back of the room, everyone would've heard it.

"Allison was dead inside too. Grimes had killed every part of her except for her will to survive."

Tears streamed down Allison's face as she lifted her head, locking eyes with Cliff. He gave her a small nod, silently acknowledging her strength. The air in the room felt raw and primal, an understanding that this was not just about a murder but about fighting against unimaginable cruelty.

The prosecutor shifted uncomfortably and glanced at the visibly affected jurors. A few women in the front row wiped away tears. Cliff had done his job. He had made them feel it.

"I have no further questions for this witness," Silver said, timing it perfectly so that the court would adjourn for the day. This was the last thing the jury would remember overnight.

Cliff stood, his legs trembling as he returned to his seat. He collapsed, drained. He'd done what he could. Now, all he could do was wait for it to sink into the hearts of twelve strangers.

At that moment, he wasn't sure what the verdict would be, but one thing was certain: the truth, the whole truth, and nothing but the truth had finally been heard.

# 15

The district attorney, Charles Reed, sat at the prosecutor's table, calmly shuffling his notes with an air of exaggerated confidence. His pale face from the previous day had been replaced by a quiet anger that simmered just below the surface.

He was obviously ready to attack, and Cliff was his intended target.

Cliff leaned back slightly in the witness chair, taking a deep breath to steady himself. He knew that Reed's cross-examination would be brutal, and he couldn't afford to underestimate him.

Even with the nervousness, he felt good about things. The missing autopsy report page was his ace in the hole. His lifeline, the one mystery Reed couldn't explain away.

But a bigger worry had kept him up the night before. What if the prosecution produced the missing page today? He could see Reed pulling it out of the file, waving it around in the air, then blowing Cliff's entire theory out of the water, cementing Allison's conviction.

Almost better that they didn't have it. Without it, Cliff could drive the point home and create reasonable doubt in the mind of the jurors.

"Mr. Ford," Reed began once the judge had taken his seat and the jury settled in. Noticeably, he did not address Cliff as "detective." A subtle tactic to diminish his authority in front of the jury.

"You testified yesterday that you believe Grimes Mansfield was already dead when Mrs. Mansfield shot him. Is that correct?"

"Yes," Cliff replied evenly, determined not to show any signs of being nervous or intimidated. "Based on the evidence I reviewed, that is my professional opinion."

Reed nodded slowly, carefully choosing his words as if savoring each one. Yet another tactic, building anticipation and leaving everyone wanting more.

"How, exactly, did Mr. Mansfield die then?"

"I don't know."

"That's right, you don't know," Reed retorted sarcastically. "But we can agree that Mr. Mansfield is indeed deceased, correct?"

"Yes, he has passed away."

He had an inkling of why Reed was asking these questions, and he was prepared for it.

"So, Mr. Ford, you admit that Mr. Mansfield died from some cause, correct?" Reed's voice grew sharper.

"Yes."

"Could two shots to the chest be enough to kill a man?"

"It is certainly possible, but Mr. Mansfield was already deceased before those shots were fired in this case."

"That's right," he spat, his words laced with sarcasm. "Your theory is based on Mrs. Mansfield's statement that her husband's body felt cold, correct?"

Cliff nodded. "That's one piece of evidence. I have also examined the autopsy report and the crime scene—"

"Oh yes. The autopsy report," Mr. Ford continued, pulling a page out of his notes. "Let's discuss that."

Cliff's heart skipped a beat as Reed stared at the paper in his hand. Could it be the missing page? A rush of dread surged through him. When Reed casually placed the paper at the back of his notes, the tension in Cliff's chest eased—slightly.

"Are you implying that Grimes Mansfield died of natural causes?"

"It's a possibility."

"Mr. Mansfield was a relatively young man," Reed continued. Something Cliff had anticipated. "There has been no evidence presented that he suffered from any heart problems or terminal conditions that could explain his premature death."

"I keep an open mind until all the facts are available. I suspect that the missing autopsy page would shed light and provide us with those facts."

This line of inquiry could pose a challenge. Reed intended to go through each potential cause of death and demonstrate just how absurd they were, hoping to lead the jury to believe that the gunshot wounds were the only plausible explanation for his death.

Cliff had struggled with this as well. If Grimes was already dead, then what caused his demise? He only had one rebuttal: the missing page from the autopsy report was the only thing that could clear up the mystery.

His throat tightened as Reed prepared to press on. He couldn't let the jury lose sight of the truth—Allison's life depended on it.

"Would you agree that he either died of natural causes, which seems improbable, or he was murdered?"

"Those are two options. Suicide would be another. Although, I've seen no evidence that Mr. Mansfield was suicidal. I only mention it as an option."

Cliff needed the jury to see him as reasonable, so they wouldn't dismiss his theory out of hand.

"Let's suppose for a moment that we stretch our imaginations and consider your theory valid. Are you saying that Mr. Mansfield may have been murdered by some means other than two shots to the chest?"

"It's conceivable, which is why I am eager to review the contents of the absent autopsy report page. It would reveal the true cause of death. The only thing I know for certain is that the gunshot wounds to the chest did not end Mr. Mansfield's life. Everything else is speculation."

"Are you saying that Mrs. Mansfield might have strangled her husband before shooting him?"

"I'm not saying that at all. There's no evidence to support such a claim. If we had the missing autopsy page, and it said that he was strangled, then shot, then that'd be something to consider."

"On the evening in question, Mrs. Mansfield was present at the scene, correct?"

"That is accurate."

"She was the only person present?"

Cliff shook his head. "I don't know that for sure."

"Are you saying she had an accomplice?"

"No. I'm saying, the real killer might've been present in the house."

Reed chuckled dismissively. Loud enough for the jury to hear it.

"During her 911 call, Mrs. Mansfield stated, 'I just killed my husband.' She confessed to murdering him, didn't she?"

"She may have assumed she killed him because she discharged the firearm."

"Or she may have known she killed him because she strangled him?"

"I don't believe … In my opinion, Mrs. Mansfield didn't know that her husband was already dead when she shot him."

Cliff reminded himself to slow down. The last thing he wanted was to get into a rapid fire back and forth. That's when mistakes happen.

"Maybe she poisoned him or suffocated him with a pillow then fired the fatal shots."

"Objection," Silver interjected firmly. "Is Mr. Reed offering expert testimony now?"

"I sustain the objection. Please ask your question."

"Isn't it true that Mrs. Mansfield was the last individual to see her husband alive?"

Cliff shook his head. "I cannot confirm that statement as fact."

"Right. You were implying earlier that someone else was present in the house on that night."

"I haven't ruled out that possibility."

"Wouldn't Mrs. Mansfield have heard an intruder if one had been present in the house?"

Cliff was glad he asked that question. He was prepared with an answer he had rehearsed in his head repeatedly.

"Mrs. Mansfield was in the torture room, having been severely beaten. She wouldn't have heard anyone enter the house if she was inside that room. Mr. Mansfield soundproofed the walls so no one would hear her screaming."

Reed ignored the comments. "That's quite a stretch of the imagination, isn't it? Are you really asking this jury to believe that an intruder broke into the house, killed Mr. Mansfield, and then Mrs. Mansfield shot him with the gun a few minutes later? How is it possible for that to happen on the same night?"

"It's possible. I've seen stranger coincidences in my years as a detective," Cliff responded calmly.

"You want us to ignore all common sense and believe that someone else could have killed him without any evidence?" Reed pressed.

"The evidence is on the missing page from the autopsy report," Cliff stated confidently.

Reed paused to look at his notes. Cliff was holding his own and things weren't going as well for Reed as he had hoped. So, Cliff decided to pile on some more.

"That's why there is reasonable doubt in my mind," Cliff said, pulling out some rehearsed lines. "I cannot say with certainty how Mr. Mansfield died. Perhaps he had a heart attack in his sleep. Maybe someone else snuck into the house and killed him while Mrs. Mansfield was stuck in that torture room. The investigator failed to explore any other possibilities. That's the problem I have with this whole investigation. You have missing evidence and an investigator who didn't do his job."

He took a deep breath to let that sink in. Avoiding looking at Bauer who was probably fuming in his seat.

Reed raised the volume and the intensity in his tone. "Mrs. Mansfield had a motive, didn't she? You yourself testified to it. She was a bitter and angry woman. She had the opportunity, correct? Her husband was asleep in their bed. And she had the means to carry out her plan, did she not? She retrieved his gun and shot him twice in the chest without even trying to hide it," Reed argued, almost angrily. "All of the elements of a crime are present."

Silver stood up and interjected, "It seems like Mr. Reed is jumping straight to his closing arguments."

The judge also had an issue with this approach.

"He has a point," the judge agreed, addressing Reed. "You asked three questions and then answered them yourself. Please ask your question and allow the witness to respond."

"Here's the main point. Mrs. Mansfield intended to kill Mr. Mansfield that night, isn't that correct?"

"Yes."

"And he is now dead!" Reed stated emphatically.

Cliff remained silent. He knew better than to answer unless asked a specific question and to keep his answers brief.

"Now, Mr. Ford, let's address the cold neck," Reed said, stepping out from behind the podium and closer to the jury. "Your conclusion relies heavily on the defendant's statement about how cold her husband's neck felt after shooting him. Isn't that subjective, Mr. Ford?"

Cliff felt a prickle of irritation rise to the surface, but he maintained a neutral expression. "It's not subjective, and it's a significant detail in my mind. From my experience, a person's body doesn't instantly cool down after death. He was sleeping under the covers. If anything, he'd feel warm to the touch."

"You must also be aware that there are countless factors that can cause a body to feel cold," Reed replied. "Right?"

Confusion furrowed Cliff's brow. "I'm not sure I understand what you mean."

Reed pounced, barely able to contain his excitement. "For example, the temperature of the room could affect how cold a body feels. Isn't it possible that Mr. Mansfield's neck felt cold because the air conditioning was blowing on him directly?"

Cliff gritted his teeth and shook his head. "No, that's not—"

"Isn't it also true that poor circulation can cause certain parts of the body to feel cold?" Reed interrupted.

"I'm not a medical professional. I cannot speak to the matter of his circulation. However, Mrs. Mansfield specifically stated to me that her husband's neck felt 'icy cold'. That sensation is often associated with a body after it has been deceased for some time. I've experienced it myself when I've touched the neck of a dead body to check for a pulse."

"What if her fingers were cold from holding the gun? She may have been nervous before shooting someone," Reed continued. "I know I would be."

Silver bolted out of his chair. "Objection. Is how Mr. Reed feels when he murders someone relevant to these proceedings?"

Laughter filled the room. Even the judge cracked a smile.

"You may answer the question, Detective Ford," the judge said. Cliff felt relieved that he called him detective again. The respite had given him time to think of a comeback.

"If her fingers were cold," Cliff responded firmly, "then his warm neck would've even felt warmer. Not colder."

"But what if she's lying? What if it was all part of her plan? To claim that her husband's neck felt cold in order to lead someone like you to believe he was already deceased?" Reed countered, exaggerating the words for effect.

"I questioned her extensively, and I believe she is telling the truth."

"But the truth remains that you don't know for sure, correct?" Reed continued. "As a self-proclaimed expert, you're grasping at straws. You're trying to convince the jury that Mrs. Mansfield didn't kill her husband because his neck felt cold, yet there could be countless logical explanations for this detail that have nothing to do with time of death. Isn't that true?"

Cliff took a deep breath to calm himself before responding. "That's not the only reason I believe Mr. Mansfield was already dead. The lack of blood at the crime scene is another crucial piece of evidence."

"You didn't answer my question. What if Mrs. Mansfield is not telling the truth, and her husband's neck wasn't cold?"

"I did answer it. After interviewing Mrs. Mansfield, I determined that she was being truthful."

"You've been wrong before, haven't you?"

"I stand by my decisions and conclusions."

"Actually, during your time in Chicago, one of the individuals you investigated and later charged with murder was awarded three million dollars for a wrongful conviction. Is that correct?"

"That is not accurate. It was later discovered that he was indeed guilty."

"So, are you saying that he did not receive a settlement from the city and that you were not suspended from your job?"

"He initially received the settlement, and I was temporarily suspended. However, I was eventually reinstated and proven right."

"The fact remains that you have been wrong before, have you not?"

"In this particular case, I'm not wrong. The evidence strongly proves that Mr. Mansfield was deceased before his wife shot him."

The grilling went on for hours. Cliff was getting tired and could tell that the jury was as well. He felt tension building in his shoulders as Reed grew more belligerent. Practically mocking Cliff.

The judge asked if Reed was about done.

"I have a few more questions, then I'm done," he answered.

His smile disappeared as he leaned his elbow on the banister in front of the jury, his voice lowering to a hushed tone as if revealing a secret to them.

"Let's focus on what we do know that's in that autopsy report, Mr. Ford. It said that Mrs. Mansfield fired two bullets into her husband's chest, correct?"

Cliff nodded in agreement. "That is correct."

"And at the time of pulling the trigger, she believed her husband was still alive, correct?"

"Yes," Cliff confirmed.

"Therefore, there is no doubt that Mrs. Mansfield believed she was shooting her living husband," Reed stated confidently.

Cliff's mouth felt dry as he answered. "Yes, she intended to kill him. But if he was already dead—"

Reed interrupted him. "So, she believed he was alive and intended to kill him and then did so. Where I come from, that's called murder."

Cliff clenched his teeth in frustration. "Yes, but—"

"Objection!"

"No further questions," Reed interjected briskly before turning his back and walking back to his table.

Cliff sat back in his chair, but the knot in his stomach remained tight. He glanced over at Allison, who sat motionless with empty eyes like the weight of the day had drained all life from her.

He had seen that same defeated expression on too many battered women before—a mix of hopelessness, fear. The faint glimmer of optimism she had felt earlier in the day was gone.

To his surprise, Silver stood up and declared, "I have no questions for this witness."

Cliff was instructed to step down from the stand. As soon as he made it back to his seat, Silver caught him off guard once again by announcing, "The defense rests."

Was that because Cliff had done so well? Silver had intended to call a psychologist as an expert witness to discuss Allison's state of mind. He obviously changed his mind.

As the courtroom emptied, Cliff couldn't shake off the feeling that buried somewhere between the air conditioning and the missing autopsy page was the truth.

Even so, Reed was right about one thing: Grimes Mansfield was dead.

And no matter what Cliff believed, no matter the missing autopsy page or the cold neck, that unchangeable fact was the biggest problem of all.

# 16

*The next day*

The courtroom was a battleground, each side fiercely defending their position. Jamie's hands gripped the edge of her seat as she watched the tension between Allison's attorney, Ty Silver, and the district attorney, Reed.

She'd faced firefights in enemy territories with less dread than this. Here, the stakes weren't for her own life—they were for Allison's future.

Words and legal arguments clashed like swords, raising the ante with every exchange. The judge tried to contain the chaos, but even his interjections added fuel to the fire. Onlookers in the courtroom were captivated by the intense back-and-forth.

Jamie's heart raced with each argument and counterpoint. In combat, she was in control of her own destiny. Here, she could only sit and watch as someone else fought for it.

To his credit, Silver fought fiercely. He defended Allison like a wolf protecting its wounded cub, refusing to let Reed corner him. He was aiming for a directed verdict, even though in his office the night before he had admitted it was a long shot. But he argued with all the passion of a boxer in the final round, trying to land that one improbable knockout blow before time ran out.

Jamie was well-versed in the workings of a courtroom, and she knew how precarious this situation was. The law didn't always prioritize truth; it was all about who could weave the most convincing story. And Reed was an expert storyteller, constructing a version of events that could easily condemn Allison if the judge and jury believed it.

Finally, the tired-looking judge leaned back in his chair, his glasses perched on the tip of his nose. Despite his fatigue, his tone commanded attention.

"That's enough," he snapped, silencing the two lawyers who were constantly talking over each other. "I will rule on the motion for a directed verdict now."

Jamie held her breath, knowing that if the judge dismissed the case before it reached the jury, Allison could walk away free today.

"The motion is denied!" he declared with certainty. His tone had a finality to it, as if he had already made up his mind about Allison's guilt.

Jamie let out a slow exhale, trying to steady herself. She had prepared for this moment with no room for emotions.

The judge continued, his tone measured. "This case will go to the jury. They are the triers of fact, and I will allow them to decide whether or not Mr. Mansfield was dead when Mrs. Mansfield shot him. If they find that he was, the question becomes whether she caused his death. If the jury finds that she didn't, that precludes a murder conviction. I will instruct them that you can't murder someone who is already dead as a matter of law."

Jamie's hopes lifted slightly until the judge added, "However, the jury may still consider attempted murder as a lesser charge."

Her jaw tightened. It didn't make sense. If you couldn't murder someone who was already dead, how could you attempt to kill them?

Rage filled her even though she understood the strategy. Judges like this one often played Solomon in the Bible, splitting the baby. It gave both sides a "win" while leaving the jury to untangle the mess.

As the bailiff brought in the jury, Jamie braced herself. Now it came down to closing arguments. The courtroom buzzed with a tense silence, electric energy as everyone watched the jury file in.

Cliff sat beside Julia, his fingers nervously tapping the arm of his chair. She appreciated that he had put his full heart into helping Allison, even if he had been skeptical at first.

Jamie's eyes drifted over to Allison. She sat quietly at the defense table, her face pale and drawn. The weight of her ordeal showed in the dark circles under her eyes. It pained Jamie that there wasn't even a quiet strength about her. She seemed resigned to her fate, even if Jamie wasn't.

Reed struck first.

"Ladies and gentlemen," he began, his authoritative voice carrying throughout the courtroom, "we've heard a lot of outlandish theories from Mr. Silver. Maybe Mr. Mansfield was dead. Maybe someone else killed him." The words dripped with sarcasm. "I commend Mr. Silver for putting up such a strong defense, but let's focus on the facts and ignore the smoke and mirrors."

Reed turned to look at the defense table and let out a noticeable chuckle. Silver clenched his jaw, clearly not finding it amusing but remained silent.

"It is undisputed that Allison Mansfield shot her husband," Reed stated. "She has already confessed to it. She wanted him dead. That shows intent."

Reed paced around the courtroom like a predator, pausing strategically as he addressed the jury without any notes, methodically laying out all the evidence.

After roughly thirty minutes of relentlessly attacking Allison and her motives, he said, "Mr. Silver claims that Mr. Mansfield was already deceased. Fine, let's consider that for a moment. Even then, Mrs. Mansfield's intention to kill remains undeniable. The law does not reward someone for poor aim or timing. If you pull the trigger with intent to kill, that is considered attempted murder—at the very least."

Jamie glanced over at the jury, trying to gauge their reactions. A few nodded subtly, while others remained stoic; some even seemed bored.

Reed continued to argue this point for longer than she had expected. He clearly was determined to secure a conviction in this case, even if it was only for the lesser charge of attempted murder. He was obviously worried that the jury may believe Cliff's compelling testimony.

The prosecutor increased his intensity, wanting to drive his point home. "The defense claims abuse and has shown you pictures of what they call a torture room. But where is the evidence that she was forced into it? Ask yourselves this: Why didn't she leave? Why didn't she call the police?

Instead, she chose to end her husband's life. That is not justifiable under the law—it is murder!"

Reed's whole body tensed, and the jury leaned in, captivated by his sudden increase in intensity.

"Mrs. Mansfield had lunch with her friends at the country club the day before, and there was no mention of abuse. She didn't ask for help or try to escape. Why?"

Jamie knew why. She had seen it countless times before. Women who were victims of abuse often lacked the strength to leave their abuser. The constant abuse drained them of their courage and left them paralyzed with fear. Only someone who had gone through it themselves could truly understand.

While she didn't want to second guess Silver, not calling the psychologist might have been a mistake. When asked about it, he felt like Cliff's testimony was compelling enough for an acquittal and didn't want to open the door for a mistake.

Reed's voice grew more fervent as he continued, urging the jury not to let sympathy sway their judgment. He reminded them that their duty was to enforce the law, and under the law, Allison Mansfield was guilty.

Jamie despised how convincing Reed was, even though she saw right through him.

His narrative was crafted for jurors who saw everything in black and white. His tone was cold and calculated, designed to resonate with those who couldn't comprehend why a victim would stay with an abusive partner.

He was relentless. "Even if everything the defense said is true, even if she was abused, there is no excuse for taking another person's life."

He gestured toward Grimes' mother, who was crying in the front row.

"She has left a mother without her only son."

He paused for effect.

"Mrs. Mansfield robbed Grimes of his future. And now she tries to paint him as a monster, smearing his name when he can no longer defend himself."

Reed straightened his tie and placed both hands on the railing in front of the jurors.

"She claims she had no other choice. I don't believe it, but perhaps you do. It's up to you to decide. But remember this: even if you feel sorry for her, we do not have the death penalty for spousal abuse in America."

Another pause. Reed was like an actor playing a role.

"She was not entitled to take the law into her own hands. There are proper channels for handling these situations. She could have filed for divorce or called the police. That's how it should've been dealt with."

He looked at Allison, his disgust evident as he pointed an accusing finger at her.

"Instead, she chose to end her sleeping husband's life with two bullets. Her own husband, who had given her so much. A nice house, expensive clothes, a car, and a bank account. And this is how she repaid him."

He lowered his voice for effect. "Grimes went to bed that night, unsuspecting. Just like every other night. Completely unaware of the danger lurking downstairs. His own wife was plotting to kill him in cold blood. Murder him with his own gun."

Jamie felt a surge of frustration. The DA was painting Allison as cold and calculated, ignoring the complexities that had been brought to light. But she had to admit, the man was good. She could see the seeds of doubt planted in the jury's minds, the legal nuances twisting the reality of the situation.

He wrapped up his summation with a final, impassioned plea. "Ladies and gentlemen, justice must be served. A guilty verdict is not just appropriate—it's required."

Ty Silver rose from his chair with steely resolve as Reed walked back to his chair. "Ladies and gentlemen." His pace to the center of the room was deliberate, his tone steady. Where Reed had been fiery, Silver was calm and methodical, his voice cutting through the tension like a knife through a cooked turkey.

"The law demands two things for a murder conviction: intent and a living victim. If either is missing, there can be no murder. And in this case, there was no life to take. Grimes Mansfield was already dead."

He let the words hang in the air before continuing. He needed to calm the emotions of the jury, and they were looking at him skeptically.

"Now, the prosecution wants you to focus on intent. But intent alone doesn't make a crime. If you fire a gun at an empty chair, intending to kill the chair, is that murder? No. It's not even attempted murder. Why not? Because the chair is not a living, human being. In this case, the defense has shown that Grimes Mansfield was dead. If you fire a gun into a lifeless body, it can't be murder."

Silver stepped closer to the jury box, lowering his voice slightly. "But let's talk about why she fired that gun. This wasn't a cold-blooded killing. This was a woman trapped in a cycle of abuse, desperate to escape. Grimes Mansfield didn't just hurt her physically—he broke her spirit. He made her believe there was no way out. That's not intent to kill. That's a cry for help."

Jamie felt a lump in her throat. Silver was equally good. He wasn't just arguing the law; he was humanizing Allison, painting her as a victim of circumstance rather than a perpetrator of violence.

"Mr. Reed asks, why didn't she call the police? Why didn't she leave? I can tell you why. Mr. Mansfield said he would kill her. Think about Mr. Reed's question for a minute. Why didn't she call a lawyer and file for divorce? Had she done so, she would've been a rich woman. The prenup agreement would've set her up for life. But she didn't trust it. She knew he would kill her. So, she did the only thing she knew to do to survive. You and I might not understand it. That's because we can't imagine the suffering he put her through."

He paused, locking eyes with each juror in turn. "Don't make her suffer even more than she already has. You have the power to make this right. The law isn't just about punishment, it's about justice. And justice demands that you find Allison Mansfield not guilty of murder. Because she didn't kill her husband. Someone else did."

Jamie watched the jury closely as Silver spent about twenty more minutes making his arguments. Rehashing Cliff's testimony. Some seemed moved, others deep in thought.

Finally, Silver finished, and the judge dismissed them to deliberate, leaving the courtroom filled with anticipation as thick as a morning fog. Jamie tried to steady her nerves.

This was it. Allison's fate was out of their hands now.

As the jury filed out, Jamie glanced at Allison, who sat silent at the defense table. Whatever the outcome, Jamie vowed she wouldn't abandon her.

If the system failed her and the jurors somehow found her guilty, even of attempted murder, Jamie would have to find another way. A burst of adrenaline shot through her, as hope began to rage, reminding her that some battles weren't won in courtrooms or through lengthy appeals. They were won by those who refused to stop fighting.

* * *

*Hours later*

The courtroom was silent as the jury filed back in, having reached a verdict in a surprisingly quick time. Silver said not to read too much into it.

Cliff and Julia sat in quiet solidarity. Allison herself sat stiffly at the defense table, her fingers intertwined tightly. The only color in her face came from the bruising under her eyes that seemed to swell since the last time Jamie saw her. From the obvious pain she was feeling.

The jury foreperson, a man in his fifties with a no-nonsense demeanor, stood and handed the verdict form to the bailiff. The bailiff delivered it to the judge, who read it silently before nodding.

"Will the defendant please rise?" the judge said.

Allison stood shakily, Silver at her side, his hand resting lightly on her arm.

The judge turned to the foreperson. "Have you reached a verdict?"

"Yes, Your Honor," the foreperson said, his voice steady but somber.

Jamie held her breath.

"In the case of the State of Florida versus Allison Mansfield, we find the defendant guilty of second-degree murder."

The words hit Jamie like a thunderclap. She felt as if the air had been knocked out of her lungs.

Cliff's head dropped slightly, his fists clenched in frustration.

Julia's eyes widened and she gasped, placing a hand over her mouth in shock.

Grimes' mother let out a wail.

Allison swayed at the defense table as if the ground beneath her was shifting. Silver tightened his grip on her arm, steadying her as he whispered something that Jamie couldn't hear.

The judge nodded gravely. "Ladies and gentlemen of the jury, thank you for your service. You are dismissed."

He then addressed the rest of the courtroom. "Sentencing will be scheduled for next month. Bailiff, take the defendant into custody. Bail is revoked. This court is adjourned."

The sound of the gavel echoed through Jamie's ears, jolting her back into reality.

As everyone began to murmur and leave, Jamie stayed seated, her eyes fixed on Allison. Silver stood by her side, speaking in hushed tones, but Allison's expression was blank and distant.

As she reached the door, Allison turned to look at Jamie and mouthed "Thank you," sending a pang of sorrow through Jamie's heart. She had to stay strong, or she would break down in tears.

"I love you," Jamie said. "It's not over yet. Don't lose hope."

Allison disappeared through the door, and Jamie made a silent vow to do whatever it took to get her out of prison. She had even considered taking Allison back to Belarus for a fresh start with a new identity and enough money to start over.

That's what she should have done. Was it too late now?

She never expected the judge to take Allison into custody before sentencing. Even if the jury found her guilty, she thought they would have more time. But now she wasn't sure how she could get her out of prison. If they were in another country, Jamie would find a way to break her out. But that wasn't an option here.

"Second-degree murder," Julia whispered after the courtroom had cleared out. Silver had gone back into the judge's chambers to meet with him and Reed.

"How is that even possible?" Julia added, tears streaming down her face.

"It doesn't matter," Cliff responded through gritted teeth. "They believed Reed's story and think intent alone is enough to pin this on her. We didn't give them another suspect to consider."

"Can we appeal?" Julia asked hopefully.

Jamie shook her head, still trying to process everything that had just happened. Appeals could take years.

"I'm sure Silver will try," Cliff replied. "But it's a long shot. Jury verdicts are rarely overturned."

"This isn't justice," Julia cried.

Cliff put his arm around his wife in comfort.

"We have to fix this," Jamie declared.

"How do we do that?" Cliff asked.

"We have to find the real killer."

# 17

It had been a long, exhausting day. A long week, actually.

Murder trials always tested Cliff's endurance, but being on the side of the defense was particularly grueling. Maybe even more so than testifying for the prosecution.

He couldn't shake the feeling that he had somehow failed Allison. For the past few hours, he had replayed his testimony in his mind, wondering if he could've said something different to alter the outcome.

A heavy knot sat at the bottom of his stomach, making it hard to eat his dinner. Maybe because he felt like he disappointed Jamie as well.

Once they put Rita to bed, Julia and Cliff collapsed onto the couch, both physically and mentally exhausted. She made him a cup of hot tea, their go-to drink for winding down after a tense day. They both needed it desperately. Despite trying not to let Rita see how stressed they were, children had a way of sensing these things and even their daughter had a hard time falling asleep.

Cliff couldn't help but feel guilty for not being fully present with his daughter tonight. His mind was consumed by the trial and its aftermath. Even as he read her a bedtime story, his thoughts were elsewhere.

After a few minutes of comfortable silence, Julia asked Cliff how he was doing.

"Tired," Cliff admitted, taking a long sip of his tea. "Frustrated. I feel bad for Allison. Spending her first night in jail will be a shock."

Julia nodded sympathetically, gazing into her own cup. Then she spoke kindly, "You did everything you could."

"But the jury didn't believe me." Cliff felt a mix of emotions bubbling up inside him, regret, sadness, and disappointment.

"That's not it," Julia said with compassion in her voice. "I can understand where the jury was coming from. It's hard to believe that someone else was in the house that night. It's too much of a stretch for them."

"I know, but I still believe there was another person there. Even if it seems like too big of a coincidence. The question is who?" Cliff said, feeling the frustration of the day rearing its ugly head again.

"You'll find out, dear. I have faith in you."

"I want to know the truth. What really happened that night? Even if it turns out Allison did do it. I owe it to Jamie."

"You always say the truth matters most," Julia said softly, her gaze steady on him. "But the truth doesn't always present itself neatly. Maybe this is one of those times where you have to dig deeper."

Julia glanced at the clock on the wall and his gaze followed hers. Already past ten o'clock. Cliff usually went to bed by now, but he knew he would likely toss and turn all night.

"Speaking of Jamie, where is she?" Cliff inquired.

After they returned home from court, Jamie disappeared into Cliff's office and hadn't come out for hours.

"I haven't seen her in at least three hours," Julia answered.

"She didn't say what she was working on. Probably something confidential, related to national security."

A few minutes later, Jamie burst into the living room with a triumphant expression and a piece of paper in her hand. Cliff had dozed off, and Julia was busy in the kitchen. He was startled and bolted up.

"Hey girl," Julia greeted Jamie cheerfully. "Do you want some tea?"

Jamie declined, already holding an energy drink in her other hand. If Cliff had one this late at night, he'd never be able to sleep. No wonder Jamie always seemed so full of energy, like she could run through a brick wall or take down a group of terrorists single-handedly.

"I was working on something," Jamie announced excitedly.

"What?" Julia asked curiously.

With dramatic flair, Jamie waved the paper towards Cliff and declared, "You'll never guess what this is."

"What is it?" Cliff asked, suddenly feeling wide awake.

Jamie handed him the paper and as he read it, his heart skipped a beat and adrenaline flooded his body.

"Is this what I think it is?" he exclaimed.

"Yep."

"What is it?" Julia asked, joining them in the living room.

Cliff let out a cry of surprise and held up the paper triumphantly. "It's the missing page from the autopsy report!"

"Shut up!" Julia exclaimed as she sat down next to him on the couch.

Cliff's mind raced as he tried to make sense of what was happening. The missing page they had been searching for was now in their possession thanks to Jamie's resourcefulness.

"How did you get this, Jamie?" Julia asked with disbelief.

Grinning, Jamie plopped into the armchair across from them and replied, "Good old Alex."

"Alex?" Cliff repeated, his confusion growing. "You mean ... Alex hacked—"

"That's exactly what I mean," Jamie said proudly. "He hacked into the coroner's computer system."

Cliff stood and began pacing, overwhelmed by this new information. "I wish you hadn't said that," he muttered. "How many laws did he break to get this piece of paper?"

"Don't worry about that," Jamie said. "Alex knows how to cover his tracks. The important thing is we have it. Have you read it yet?"

Cliff realized that he had been so focused on finally finding the missing page that he hadn't actually read its contents. As he perused through it, his jaw dropped in shock.

*Cause of death: Homicide*

*Time of death: 10:00-11:00 p.m.*

The coroner had made several notes on the page. Grimes suffered a blow to the right side of his head and also had a crushed windpipe. The cause of death could not be definitively determined. However, the coroner clearly stated that the gunshot wounds to the chest were inflicted post-mortem.

"You were right, Cliff," Jamie declared triumphantly. "The coroner's report supports your theory. Grimes was already dead when Allison shot him."

Cliff couldn't believe what he was reading, even though it confirmed his initial theory.

"The page was deliberately deleted from the records," Jamie explained further, "but Alex found it on the hard drive since it hadn't been properly erased. He said someone intentionally removed that page."

*The killer?*

"May I see it?" Julia asked.

Cliff handed her the paper, and after reading it, Julia looked up and said, "This is good news, isn't it?"

"It's great news," Jamie exclaimed. "Allison didn't kill Grimes. He was already dead. Look at the time of death. Between ten and eleven o'clock. Six hours before Allison shot him. Allison didn't make the 911 call until after four in the morning. The judge has to dismiss the charges now."

Julia leaned forward on the couch, her eyes wide as she read it again. Her hand flew to her mouth. "Oh, my goodness. This is unbelievable."

Jamie's smile faded as she said, "What's wrong, Cliff? You look like you just lost your best friend. I thought you'd be happy. This is exactly what we need to get Allison's conviction overturned, right?"

"Yes and no," Cliff responded, still staring off at the ceiling. "This doesn't prove that Allison didn't kill Grimes. He was hit in the head and his windpipe crushed before she even pulled the trigger. But ..."

"But what?"

"I'm not so sure this helps Allison."

"Why not?"

"Well, for starters, we can't explain how we got this report. What Alex did is illegal. We're all accomplices now."

Jamie furrowed her brow in concern. "Like I said, Alex is too good at covering his tracks. They'll never be able to trace it back to us."

"That may be true, but I can't just hand this over to Silver with no explanation as to how I obtained it," Cliff stated firmly.

"You could say someone left it on your doorstep," Jamie suggested.

Cliff shook his head. "That would be lying, and I can't do that under oath in front of a judge. Which is where we want this to end up."

Jamie let out a frustrated sigh. "It's so much simpler for me out in the field. I make judgment calls based on life-or-death situations. Out there, I am the judge and jury."

"But our justice system relies on truth and honesty," Cliff reminded her. "If we lie or cheat to secure justice, then we're no better than the criminals we're fighting against."

"I know, I know," Jamie grumbled. "But sometimes the ends justify the means. If breaking the law in another country means saving lives and taking down dangerous criminals, then I'll do it without hesitation."

Cliff couldn't help but feel conflicted. On the one hand, using this report could secure Allison's freedom and potentially save her life. But on the other hand, it went against everything he believed in and could ultimately land them all in jail.

"What if we anonymously mailed it to Silver?" Julia suggested.

Jamie suddenly snatched the report from Cliff's hands. "I'll take care of it myself. I'll break into Silver's office and leave it on his desk, so he sees it first thing in the morning. He'll never suspect a thing."

Cliff shook his head, trying to process what Jamie had just told him. "I'm going to pretend I didn't hear that," he said.

"I agree. The less you know, the better," Jamie replied.

She looked like she was about to leave and go take care of the situation herself.

"But what if someone sees you? Or there's a security camera?" Cliff questioned.

Jamie let out a dismissive laugh. "I could sneak into Fort Knox tonight without anyone noticing if I wanted to. Alex can handle taking care of the cameras. I'll be in and out before anyone knows what happened."

"That's all well and good, but we need a clean copy of the page without our fingerprints on it," Cliff pointed out.

He couldn't believe he was aiding and abetting her in committing a crime.

"I'll print out another one. And I'll wear gloves. This isn't my first rodeo," Jamie said as she turned towards the office to carry out her plan.

"Wait, let's think this through," Cliff interjected.

Jamie spun around on her heel and walked back into the room. "What's there to think about?" she retorted. "I'll plant the page and make sure it doesn't trace back to either of us. Reed won't suspect you if he finds out the page was planted in Silver's office. Why would he? You're not lying, just withholding information. Surely, you don't have an issue with that."

"No, I don't."

"Then what's the problem?"

"The problem is we have to make sure this clears Allison's name completely. This page only proves that Grimes was already dead when she shot him. It doesn't rule out the possibility that she hit him on the head and strangled him beforehand. The jury could easily make that assumption. And you know Reed will make that point," Cliff explained.

Jamie furrowed her brow and leaned back in her chair. "I see your point. So, what do we do? Just sit on it?"

"The judge won't consider it unless we can prove it's real. If we give this to Silver, he'll give it to the prosecution. They'll give it to Bauer. I don't trust him to investigate it properly. I want to do it myself. I want to prove it's authentic."

"Can't the coroner verify his own handwriting?" Julia suggested. "Or we could bring in a handwriting expert to examine it."

"That's the right idea, Julia," Cliff said. "That's what I plan on doing. I'll go to the coroner's office tomorrow and get him to verify his signature. See if he remembers the autopsy. If I can prove this is real, then the judge will have to reopen the trial in order for us to present new evidence. But I also need to make sure it doesn't make Allison look more guilty."

"It doesn't seem like something Allison would do," Julia said. "She's not physically capable of bludgeoning and strangling someone. And why would she choose to do that instead of just shooting him?"

"Julia, can I see that autopsy report again?" Cliff asked.

Julia handed it to him, and he carefully studied the details. Something about the description of the cause of death caught his attention.

"Wait a minute," Cliff muttered. "The coroner stated that Grimes' windpipe was crushed."

"That's what I'm saying," Julia replied. "Allison is a petite girl."

"It doesn't take much force to crush a windpipe," Jamie chimed in. "Trust me, I know."

Cliff's eyes scanned the report again. His heart quickened as a detail leapt out at him. "The crush marks on his neck ... these aren't from Allison. They're too faint, too precise. This wasn't a struggle. It was a professional kill. Allison wouldn't know how to crush a man's windpipe without leaving any marks."

"No, she wouldn't. That's more evidence that she's innocent," Jamie said.

"And the fatal blow to the head was powerful enough to crush his skull."

"It takes some serious strength to do that," Jamie said. "Trust me, I know."

He turned back to Jamie and Julia, resolve hardening in his voice.

"I need more," Cliff said. "This isn't enough to get a judge to overturn a conviction."

"Allison didn't kill Grimes," Julia said. "I'm sure of it. And I have good instincts."

Cliff nodded. "Even if Allison could somehow kill Grimes without leaving a mark, there's no way she could delete this page off the coroner's computer. There's more to this page than her guilt or innocence. It exposes a cover-up. Someone went to a lot of trouble to erase this evidence, and we need to figure out why."

"Tell me what to do and I'll do it," Jamie said.

"Me too," Julia said.

Cliff walked to the window, staring into the darkness beyond.

For a brief moment, he thought he saw something move in the shadows. His heart skipped a beat. He narrowed his eyes, straining to see.

Nothing. Just the still night.

But his instincts told him otherwise.

"What is it, Cliff?" Julia's voice broke the silence.

"I thought I saw somebody out there."

Jamie didn't hesitate. She bolted for the door, disappearing into the night. Moments later, she returned, her expression fraught with concern.

"I didn't see anyone, but I heard a car engine rev up and speed away."

"I know I saw something move." Cliff's voice was firm.

"They're watching us," Jamie said, her tone sharper now.

Julia's hand tightened on Cliff's arm. "What do we do?"

Cliff glanced at Jamie, then back into the shadows. Someone was out there watching, waiting.

"Okay. Now we know. Somebody was in the house that night. Whoever it was killed Grimes and then covered it up. Now he's watching us."

"Don't forget that someone broke into our office," Julia said. "We know Allison didn't do that."

"Everything is related. Somebody is nervous."

"He's afraid we won't drop it," Jamie said.

"He should be afraid. I won't drop it. Not until Allison is free, and he's the one behind bars."

# 18

*The next morning*

Cliff sat at his desk, sipping his second cup of coffee and poring over his notes from Allison's file. Jamie burst into his office, her phone gripped tightly in her hand like a weapon.

"Cliff, we've got another lead," she said, her voice brimming with urgency.

He'd been awake since the early hours of the morning, unable to sleep. But he felt alive and energized, the familiar thrill of tracking down a murderer flooded back to him from his days as a detective in Chicago.

"What's the lead?" he asked.

"Grimes was having an affair!" she exclaimed.

The words hit Cliff like a surge of electricity, sending adrenaline coursing through his body like a dozen of Jamie's energy drinks.

"How do you know?" he asked.

"Alex hacked into Grimes's phone," Jamie informed him.

Cliff let out a yelp in disbelief, trying to process this new information.

"How did Alex get access to Grimes's phone?" Julia walked in at that moment, handing Cliff another mug of hot coffee.

"Not the actual phone, just the records," Jamie clarified.

Cliff arched an eyebrow. "How?"

"It's better not to ask," Jamie replied with a smirk. "The important thing is that we have all of Grimes's calls and texts."

"So, who was he having an affair with?" Cliff questioned, taking a deep sip of his coffee and reveling in the rush of caffeine that further heightened his already sharp senses.

Jamie shook her head. "We don't have a name for the woman yet. She was using a burner phone. But Alex managed to trace the location of the calls and texts based on cell tower data."

"Where were they together?"

"At a few different locations. One by a hotel in the downtown area, and another near a marina. Grimes owns a yacht there. And sometimes her phone was traced to his house."

"That scoundrel!" Julia exclaimed with disgust. "He betrayed Allison right under her nose. They may have even slept together in their own bed."

Julia suddenly covered her mouth with her hand, gasping at the thought. "Do you think they used the torture room?"

"I wouldn't put it past him," Jamie replied in a serious tone. "The texts are explicit. Grimes had some dark tendencies, as we know. Alex sent me copies. I'll print them out for you."

Cliff nodded, already considering how this new information could be useful.

"An affair opens up so many possibilities," he mused aloud. "The killer could be the woman's husband or lover, or even the woman herself. It's also possible that someone hired a hitman on behalf of the woman's significant other."

"Exactly," Jamie agreed, rubbing her temples as if she had a headache. It seemed like she hadn't gotten much sleep either. Julia noticed and offered to make her a cup of coffee, but she declined and asked for an energy drink instead.

Julia disappeared out the door.

"Does Alex have any more information for us?" Cliff asked.

Jamie shook her head. "I don't believe so. This is all I could come up with."

"I wish we had known this earlier."

"I know, I'm sorry. Alex has been tied up on a secret CIA mission. He didn't really have time to do this for me, but after Allison was convicted, I made it clear that he had no choice."

"At least we have it now. Even if it's too late to stop the conviction."

Julia returned with the energy drink. Jamie popped it open and drank it down in a few gulps. "Please convey our thanks to Alex," Julia said. "This is wonderful news for Allison."

Cliff shook his head, causing Julia's eyes to widen in surprise.

"What's the matter?" she asked.

"This gives Allison another potential motive besides just money," he explained. "It opens up the possibility for the prosecution to portray her as a jealous wife seeking revenge. Motive is a key factor that convinces judges and juries of guilt. Once they believe you're guilty, they see everything through that lens."

"But wouldn't her husband having an affair make her more sympathetic?" Julia countered.

"No. The system wants someone to be held responsible for Grimes' death," Cliff said. "That's how it works. The judge may feel sorry for her, but he could also see it as the reason why she killed her husband."

"Well, if I were the judge and found out about the affair, I would definitely side with Allison," Julia stated firmly. "An affair could drive anyone to commit murder."

"Alex knows that if he ever has an affair on me, he's a dead man," Jamie chimed in jokingly with a hint of bitterness in her voice.

"You can always use the Allison defense," Cliff quipped back. "After you shoot him, claim his neck was cold, and I'll even testify on your behalf."

She waved off the joke with a mischievous grin. "Don't worry about me," she said. "They'd never find his body."

"Alex adores you," Julia insisted. "He would never do that to you."

"I'm just saying, he better not," Jamie responded.

"I would never do that to you," Cliff reassured Julia lovingly. "I adore you too much."

"Thank you, honey. And just so you know, if you ever did cheat on me, I always have Jamie to take care of it and dispose of your body."

"You can count on me, girl," Jamie chimed in. "We have to stick together and keep our men in line."

"Can we please get back to the matter at hand?" Cliff interjected abruptly, trying to change the subject before it got any more uncomfortable.

Julia chuckled but agreed with Cliff's serious tone. "Of course, back to business," she said, her voice softening. "What's our next move?"

"First, we need to handle this autopsy report. I want to give it to Silver, but we can't just hand it over," Cliff explained. "If I'm asked, I need to be able to honestly say that I don't know who gave it to me."

"How are you going to do that?" Jamie inquired.

"Here's what I want you and Julia to do. Go around back, take a copy of the autopsy report with you, and one of you leave it by the back door. I'll find it there. If anyone asks, I can say that I don't know who put it there. And that would be the truth. I won't know which one of you left it."

Julia smiled. "So technically, you wouldn't be lying."

"Brilliant," Jamie praised. "Should we use a copy without fingerprints?"

"It doesn't matter," Cliff nonchalantly shrugged his shoulders. "We can just say all three of us saw it and touched it. That's believable."

"Good idea, and I'll make sure to leave a copy of the phone records with the autopsy report," Jamie added.

"I'm not sure what I'm going to do with them yet, but I want to have that option. I might just confront our good friend Detective Bauer about Grimes's affair and see how he reacts. I want to know if he already knows about it. He does if he pulled his phone records."

"I'm suspicious of him," Jamie stated firmly. "He lied to us."

"The question is why," Cliff said. "Did he remove the autopsy page from the file or was it missing when he got it?"

"Either way, he covered it up."

"There could be any number of reasons why," Cliff reasoned.

"He didn't want to go to all the effort of tracking down the real culprit," Jamie said. "He went for the low-hanging-fruit."

"Perhaps. Detectives are under a lot of pressure to wrap up cases quickly. Allison's conviction was a sure thing. In Bauer's defense, it's even possible that he went to his lieutenant, who advised him to take the path of least resistance and hide any information that could complicate Allison's prosecution. Solving a high-profile case and pinning guilt on a wealthy gold-digger made the entire department look good."

"I can't believe you're defending him," Jamie scoffed.

"I'm not necessarily defending him. I have my suspicions as well. For instance, I can see where he could've missed the crushed windpipe, but how did he miss the blow to the head?"

"He didn't. He saw it and removed the pictures from the file."

"We don't know for sure that he took pictures," Cliff said. "If he did, why would he pull those from the file? If anything, the blow to the head strengthens the case against Allison."

"Maybe he saw the autopsy report and came to the same conclusion we came to. That Allison wasn't sophisticated enough to crush Grimes's windpipe."

"That's why I want to talk to the coroner. Too many *maybes* to draw any conclusions. We'll take this one step at a time."

"Right. Let's go plant that information on the back porch," Julia said to Jamie, tugging on her arm.

Cliff handed Jamie the copy of the autopsy page.

"This is so exciting," Julia said with a giggle. "It's like we're real spies. We need to talk about which one of us is going to leave it on the back patio."

She took Jamie's hand and led her out of the office. They returned a few minutes later and Julia seemed pleased with herself. Cliff figured by the satisfied look on her face that she was the one who left the papers on the doorstep. The few times they had played poker, he always knew when she had a good hand and when she was bluffing.

He smiled at her admirably. Poker wasn't her game, but she always managed to win at being adorable. Times like this made him realize how much he loved her Cuban passion.

"It's done," Jamie said as she leaned against the desk. "What's next, boss?"

Cliff took a moment to gather his thoughts before replying, "First, I'm going to visit the coroner and have him confirm that it's his signature on the page. I also want to see if he knows how it went missing and if he remembers performing the autopsy. Then I'll head to the funeral home and talk to the person who worked on Grimes's body. See if he remembers anything. He would've noticed the blow to the head when he prepared the body for cremation."

"Silver said that the coroner didn't remember because he did so many autopsies that he couldn't recall them all," Jamie said.

"I want to look him in the eye and see if he's lying. For all I know, he might be a part of the cover up."

"Good idea."

"Jamie, you and Julia go down to the area where the cell phones were pinged and look around. Take a picture of Grimes with you and canvas the area to see if anyone saw anything."

"We're on it," Jamie said. "If she met him at the marina, someone there might've seen them together—dock workers, restaurant staff, anyone. I'm going to go take a shower and get dressed and have another energy drink and a power bar."

She disappeared out of the room.

"What about Mrs. Plumley?" Julia asked.

Cliff let out a loud moan. "I know. I haven't forgotten about her."

"We promised we'd come back to Key West as soon as the trial was over."

"It'll have to wait. This is more pressing."

Cliff felt the urgency. If a killer was watching their house, his wife and daughter's lives were in danger.

Julia came over and tenderly kissed Cliff's ear. "Be careful," she whispered, barely audible.

Her lips brushed against his ear, but her words carried a chilling weight. A shiver ran down Cliff's spine, not from her touch but from the foreboding feeling that he couldn't quite put into words—danger?

She reminded him that he needed to be cautious. He wasn't just a private investigator chasing after a cat; this was real life. He was once again tracking someone who had already killed and could potentially strike again. Someone who lurked outside his home in the dark of night.

After Julia and Jamie left, Cliff went out onto the back deck to take in the warm morning air. He scanned his surroundings to ensure no one was watching him.

Feeling uneasy, Cliff glanced toward the tree line where he thought he saw movement. It could have been just the branches swaying in the breeze, but his instincts were on high alert. The sidearm against his hip under his shirt brought him some comfort.

After a few minutes lost in thought, Cliff gathered the autopsy report and phone records before heading back inside. He loaded the file in his briefcase and went to get into his car. A sense of determination washed over him. A feeling that had become second nature during his time in Chicago.

After pulling out of the garage, he looked around once more to check for any potential threats, instinctively placing his hand on his gun. A habit he had picked up in Chicago, one that he would repeat multiple times before lunch.

The gun served as a grounding reminder, a familiar partner in the ongoing pursuit. This was no longer just an investigation; it had turned into a hunt.

# 19

The coroner's office was all too familiar to Cliff.

As soon as he entered, the sharp smell of antiseptic assaulted his senses, overpowering any lingering scent of death in the basement of the government building. The sophisticated refrigeration systems kept the entire floor cooled to a chilly fifty-five degrees, and thirty-six inside the morgue where the bodies were stored.

The cold air made him shiver and immediately dried up the perspiration under his shirt and on his brow. He stood in the lobby, able to see through the double doors into the main room where standard equipment filled the area: walk-in refrigerators, small door refrigerators, lab freezers, and cadaver lockers.

Above, harsh fluorescent lights flickered and cast a sterile light over the white-tiled floor and metallic tables. Every step echoed loudly in the large space, adding to the eerie atmosphere.

This particular facility was bigger than most but smaller than Chicago's massive morgue, where bodies would often stack up on Monday mornings after a particularly violent weekend. No matter how many times he visited these places, something oppressive about them made Cliff's neck hair stand on end. He felt a knot of tension form in his stomach; a feeling he still hadn't gotten used to even after all these years.

The coroner emerged from a hallway. A thin, middle-aged man. His hair was thin as well but showed no signs of gray. His eyes held weariness from years of examining bodies and trying to make sense of death.

Cliff introduced himself and displayed both his private investigator card and detective badge from his wallet, making sure to hide most of the PI card with his thumb. The coroner glanced at the badge without much reaction before leading Cliff to his office.

He held a clipboard in hand, probably filled with notes from a recent autopsy. After sitting down in his modest and worn office chair, he tapped his fingers on the edge of his desk in a restless rhythm, his gaze darting toward the clock on the wall more than once, trying to be polite, but clearly bothered by the intrusion.

The hum of the refrigeration system was more prevalent there and overpowered the silence between them. It thrummed in Cliff's ears like a faint, persistent whisper, as if the dead themselves were trying to speak over the din.

Cliff shook off the thought and sat back in his chair, trying to make himself comfortable in the medicinal chill he couldn't imagine working in ten hours a day, six days a week.

"Detective Ford," Yun Young said, first name pronounced like John. "How can I help you today?"

Cliff didn't correct Young when he called him detective, hoping he would be more cooperative if he thought Cliff was currently one. If anyone ever questioned his use of the title, he'd play ignorant. Technically, he never said he was a detective now.

"You performed an autopsy over a year ago," Cliff began. "On Grimes Mansfield. Do you remember it?"

The coroner chuckled. "I've performed quite a few since then, but I am familiar with that case due to its media coverage. I also received a request from Mrs. Mansfield's attorney about a missing page from the autopsy report. I looked it up and confirmed it is indeed missing."

"I have that missing page," Cliff revealed.

Young raised an eyebrow in surprise. Cliff handed him a copy of the document, and he scrutinized it closely.

"Is that your signature?" Cliff inquired. "I wanted to make sure it was genuine."

The coroner's eyes scanned over the paper a second time, and Cliff could see recognition dawn in his expression before he nodded. "Yes, it is my signature."

The surprise in his voice and his mannerisms indicated that he had not been the one who tampered with the document.

"Do you recall performing an autopsy on the deceased?" Cliff asked.

Young leaned forward in his chair, still staring at the page, obviously trying to make some sense of it.

"After doing so many autopsies, they all start to blend together. But now that I'm looking at it again, I do remember this one. The victim was shot after he was already dead, approximately six hours post-mortem. It's not something I encounter often in my line of work. So yes, it stands out, and I do remember it now."

A shiver ran down Cliff's spine and not from the cold environment. He knew the page was authentic since it came from Alex. But now, with the coroner's confirmation, he had something concrete to take to Silver.

He probed further. "Can you explain how that page could have vanished from your records?"

A dark expression came over the coroner's face and his eyes glassed over. "I have no explanation for that. On occasion, we have had files accidentally deleted or lost. But never just one page. In those situations, I refer to my notes which are also mysteriously missing."

This was new information to Cliff.

One of his colleagues appeared at the door and beckoned him away. A hearse had arrived to collect a body. "If you'll excuse me for a moment," the coroner said as he left the office.

Left alone, Cliff realized how easy it'd be for someone to tamper with the evidence. He was left unsupervised for nearly twenty minutes, and the computer screen remained open the entire time. If he had wanted to, he could have deleted a page or altered a file.

The long wall of filing cabinets likely held the coroner's notes. It wouldn't take much effort for someone to remove one of them.

When Young returned, Cliff asked a few more questions. As it became clear that he had gathered all the information he could from him, Cliff thanked him and left with more than he had hoped for.

Now he could prove in a court of law that Grimes was dead when Allison shot him. He also had a plausible explanation for the disappearance of the document. Anyone could've come in the coroner's office and deleted it when Young wasn't looking.

Well ... not anyone. No, it had to be someone who belonged there—or someone with enough clout to fake it.

Who could waltz into a government building and tamper with evidence when the coroner wasn't looking? Likely the same person resourceful enough to break into his office and brazen enough to stake out his home in the dark of night.

Find that person and he'd likely solve this case.

How much time did he have?

His gut instinct warned him that danger loomed over his family, a threat that grew stronger with each passing moment.

Stepping out into the suffocating heat of Miami, he felt the lingering chill of the coroner's office still clinging to his skin. Yet there was something else, a tingling sensation down his spine that hinted at a darker truth just beyond his reach.

The killer's looming shadow seemed to stretch even further now, his presence more ominous with every new secret uncovered. The thought sent his emotions spiraling as he realized he'd have to delve deeper into the twisted mind of a murderer. Something he did regularly in Chicago but hadn't had to do for several months now.

What other secrets was the killer still hiding? And how far would he go to keep them buried?

* * *

*Later that night*

Cliff, Julia, and Jamie sat around the kitchen table, each nursing a beverage of choice. The iced tea in front of Cliff had grown lukewarm, the ice long since melted. Julia's fingers curled around her mug of hot tea, though she hadn't taken a sip in several minutes, and it probably wasn't hot anymore.

Jamie had a concoction of coke and an energy drink, mixed in the blender with blueberries, green superfood, a banana, creatine, and a chocolate protein powder. Seemingly enough fuel to power a diesel engine. A discolored sludge she insisted was "fuel for champions."

The conversation had grown intense as they discussed the day's events, but the tension had lessened some as they covered everything. The clock on the wall ticked away the seconds and the hour was late, but none of them seemed ready to sleep.

"So," Cliff said, his voice cutting through the tiredness he felt, "to recap, the coroner confirmed the authenticity of the autopsy page. He stated that the blow to the head didn't break the skin and was barely noticeable. The funeral home director said that he didn't notice it. That's why Bauer missed it. I can see why he didn't see the crushed windpipe either."

He glanced over his notes.

"There's also the mystery blonde wearing a wig who was seen with Grimes multiple times at the marina," Cliff continued. "Good job, ladies, finding that eyewitness."

"Most certainly Grimes's paramour," Julia interjected. "The wig was to conceal her identity although the woman at the marina felt certain she would recognize her if she saw her again."

Cliff nodded. "I don't think she'll be showing up at that marina any time soon. I wish she would. Unfortunately, we don't know her identity or how to find her."

"I can imagine she's been living in fear," Jamie chimed in. "Her lover was murdered and every knock on her door probably made her heart race, thinking the police were on to her. We know from text messages between her and Grimes that she was also married. She's probably petrified that her husband will find out about the affair."

"Or maybe he already knows about it," Julia said. "And he's the one who killed Grimes."

Cliff agreed. It seemed like the best investigative thread to pursue. He had a list of suspects on his notepad. First on the list was the "lover's husband." He glanced down at the blank space next to it. He needed a name to put there.

"The blonde didn't have to worry about the police," Cliff said. "Bauer had tunnel vision and didn't even think to look for any other possible suspects."

"He had Allison signed, sealed, and delivered for a conviction," Jamie said with a hint of bitterness behind the words.

"The lover is lucky I wasn't the investigator," Cliff said. "I would've at least considered it. A wife kills her husband in his sleep, the first thing I think of is that there's another woman in the picture."

"If we find the blonde, we get more answers," Jamie said, stating the obvious.

Julia tapped her fingers against her mug, her forehead creased in thought. "But how do we even begin to track her down? It seems like we're chasing a ghost."

"That's why it's called an investigation," Cliff said. "It's hardly ever easy."

"Who do you think was tailing us today?" Julia asked.

Jamie had spotted the car following them on their way to the marina.

"I don't know. But I have my suspicions. I wish you had gotten close enough to identify him," Cliff said.

"Are you positive it's a man?" Julia asked. "Could it have been the blonde? We didn't get a good look at the driver."

"It's possible," Cliff replied. "But my gut tells me she's gone into hiding. I don't see her as the murderer. Why would she kill her wealthy boyfriend? Nothing in their texts suggested any issues between them. I also didn't see any blondes at the trial or lurking around outside. That's something I always keep an eye out for. Murderers often return to the scene of the crime or show up at trials. I checked every day for anyone who seemed suspicious."

"I don't remember noticing any standout blondes, except for you, Jamie," Julia said, with a faint smile that she matched.

"My guess is that whoever was following you is the killer," Cliff said. "The husband seems like a good suspect."

"Why would he follow us?" Julia asked. "He's off the hook."

"Maybe he doesn't think he is. He's nervous and wants to see if we're still investigating. Even though Allison was convicted, he's still concerned that he could get caught if we don't drop it."

"He should be worried," Jamie said, emphatically. "We aren't going to drop it."

"How skilled was the tail?" Cliff asked.

Jamie took a big gulp of her drink and set the glass down with a thud. "The tail was amateur, but persistent. Whoever it was, they weren't trying to engage. They were just keeping tabs on us. Before I could confront him, he took off."

She took another swig then explained the tactics she used to expose the tail.

"I made four consecutive right turns. That's the best way to out somebody. When he pulled up to the stop sign right before the fourth right, he must've become suspicious, because he turned left and disappeared. If he hadn't, I would've nailed him. As it is, all I have is a description of the car."

"We'll set a trap for the tail. Hopefully, he'll keep trying to follow us," Cliff said.

"If he does, I'll spot him," Jamie said.

"In the meantime, we need to recheck Grimes' financial records. Knowing Grimes, he was probably lavishing her with gifts. There might be a paper trail we can follow."

"Good idea." Jamie leaned back in her chair, crossing her arms. "A florist might've delivered flowers giving us an address. A jeweler might remember something. Grimes might've had her name engraved on a bracelet or something."

"Exactly. We'll get started on it first thing in the morning."

Jamie stood, stretching her arms above her head. "Well, on that note, I'm calling it a night. Don't stay up too late, old man," she teased, smirking at Cliff.

"You're the one going to bed first, Jamie," he quipped, watching her disappear down the hallway with a dismissive wave meant for him.

The room fell quiet again. Cliff reached for his iced tea, taking a long sip despite its tepid temperature. His mind buzzed with the day's revelations, the threads of the case tangling and unraveling in equal measure.

Julia stood and placed her mug in the sink, then turned to him. "You coming to bed?"

"In a minute," Cliff replied. "I need to think."

She hesitated, then leaned down to kiss his forehead. "Don't stay up too late. You need your rest. You'll figure it out eventually. You always do."

That wasn't exactly true. Though he had a stellar success rate in Chicago, he mostly remembered the murders that were still unsolved.

Cliff watched his wife retreat upstairs, the sound of her footsteps fading into the distance. He sat alone at the table and stared down at his notepad. He began to write down ideas on how to find the blonde. When he finished, he looked over the list of suspects again.

A scenario started to form in his mind causing his pulse to race. A theory. Something he couldn't talk about but made sense to him as an investigator. If he was right, the trail lay before him, but almost certainly paved with uncertainty and danger.

He stood and his heart suddenly pounded as he turned off the lights and stalked to each window, peering out into the darkness for any signs of lurking threats. Sweat beaded on his forehead as he tried to shake off the feeling of being watched.

With a weary sigh, he rubbed a hand over his face before turning on a light in the kitchen, knowing that Jamie might need it in the middle of the night.

Cliff went upstairs and fell into bed, but sleep was elusive. Balancing on a precipice of exhaustion and determination, he stared at the ceiling and willed himself to find some peace amidst the chaos of his thoughts. But they refused to calm, tangled in a web of unanswered questions and fears of never finding the truth or the identity of the blonde.

Eventually, he drifted off to sleep. A couple hours later, he was startled awake by a faint noise downstairs.

He bolted up in his bed. Listening carefully.

Was he hearing things in his sleep? Was his mind playing tricks on him?

He heard it again. Louder this time. Coming from downstairs.

Instinct kicked in immediately. He regretted that his gun was in the safe downstairs in his office.

He slithered out of bed, moving carefully so he wouldn't wake Julia. He eased the door open and stepped into the darkened hallway that led to the landing at the top of the stairs.

The house was still, but the unease in his gut told him something was wrong.

He peered over the landing but didn't have a good angle to see anything. A sound was coming from the kitchen area.

As he crept down the stairs, voices drifted up to meet him. Two. Jamie's familiar voice mingled with that of another man's. He couldn't make out what they were saying.

He felt momentary relief as he deduced that Jamie was talking to Alex on the phone. He decided to continue down the stairs so he could say hello to him.

As he got to the bottom of the stairs, he realized it wasn't Alex. The man's familiar voice was coming from inside the house and his tone was threatening.

Too late to turn back now.

The man saw him.

Their eyes met.

The detective—Bauer.

With a gun in his hand, held steady, and aimed directly at Jamie.

# 20

As Cliff tried to assess the situation, his heartbeat rang loudly in his ears as fear washed over him like water from a cold shower.

Jamie stood calmly in the space between the living room and kitchen with a gun pointed at her, her body language relaxed as if a life-or-death situation was commonplace for her.

Which it was, but why wasn't she taking any action?

Jamie was once known as the most lethal CIA operative in the world, a former top assassin who could easily disarm the detective. However, she remained motionless, even as Bauer had turned the gun on Cliff.

The creak of the wood on the stairs had betrayed his presence. Bauer's eyes were filled with fire. "Don't try anything foolish, Ford, or you're a dead man," he barked, his voice cold and menacing.

Slowly, Cliff raised his hands in a non-threatening manner. "Okay, let's not do anything stupid."

Jamie watched Bauer with casual intensity. Her words matched her demeanor.

"Come join us, Cliff?" she said, in a most nonchalant and confident tone. "The detective and I were about to have an interesting conversation."

Bauer's mouth curled into a twisted smirk, the kind of arrogant grin that told Cliff he was confident as well.

"Yes, little lady, we do need to have that conversation. Why couldn't you two leave well enough alone? Ford, I saw you at the coroner's office. What were you doing there?"

Before Cliff could answer, he pointed his finger at Jamie.

"I saw you drive down to the marina where Grimes had his yacht. What business do you have at the marina?"

With a sharp and taunting tone, Jamie retorted, "How long was your wife having an affair with Grimes?"

The tension in the air raised considerably, if that were even possible.

The detective's demeanor shifted in an instant, the smirk morphing into a scowl of pure venom. Telling Cliff everything he needed to know.

"How did you know about—" Bauer cut off his words, bit his lip, then sneered, his eyes dark and burning with resentment.

"My wife wasn't having an affair with Grimes," he said, without any real conviction in his voice. "I have no idea where you got that information."

"Is that why you killed him?" Jamie asked.

"I didn't kill Grimes. Your girl did it. Old news. The jury found her guilty."

Even Cliff could tell he was lying through his teeth.

In fact, Cliff had figured out the truth the night before. It made perfect sense that Bauer would be the one to remove the autopsy page from the file. He was the most plausible one to gain access to the coroner's computer.

Cliff had even written Bauer's name on his notepad the night before next to 'lover's husband,' with a question mark next to it. But now, there were no more questions left.

"Drop the pretense, Bauer," Jamie said, smugly. "We know everything. Grimes was doing your wife."

Jamie was baiting him, almost mocking him, hoping to get under his skin. Get him to incriminate himself. Cliff worried that she might push him too far and end up getting shot.

"I bet you were shocked when you arrived at the crime scene and realized Allison had shot him," Jamie continued.

Bauer chuckled, his eyes glancing up at the ceiling as if recalling that fateful night.

"Were you going to kill Allison too? I think so. But she was down in the torture room? You didn't know about that room, did you? Did you know that your wife went there with Grimes? Who knows what kind of depraved things they did together."

*What are you doing, Jamie? Don't push him too far.*

No verbal response from Bauer, although the anger on his face from the contorted lips and tense brow betrayed him.

"You somehow manipulated things so that you got assigned to the murder," Jamie said. "I'm sure it wasn't that hard. You have connections. But Allison shooting Grimes came with complications. You had to make the evidence fit."

Cliff decided to interject himself into the conversation, hoping to distract Bauer long enough for Jamie to take action. He could see her plan and supported it. As long as they kept Bauer engaged in conversation, he would not pull the trigger. Not until he knew how much they had uncovered.

"You thought Allison had made things easier for you by shooting him, but she actually made it more complicated," Cliff said, smartly. "The autopsy report was a problem. It showed that the victim was already dead when she shot him. You hadn't anticipated me figuring that out."

"You stuck your nose where it didn't belong, Ford," Bauer spat.

"That's why you were following us," Jamie interjected. "That's why you're here tonight. We were getting too close to the truth. So, you came here to kill us both."

Cliff's mind raced as he realized the detective's plan. A perfect storm of lies, arrogance, and cold-blooded murder.

But what terrified Cliff the most were Bauer's next confirming words.

"Doesn't matter now," the detective said, his voice dripping with malice. "I'll kill you both, and then I'll get assigned to investigate your deaths as well. Maybe I'll even find a way to pin it on Allison. She could easily hire a hitman from prison. No one will suspect a thing."

And there they had it. The confession Jamie was pressing for. But would it hold up in a court of law? Bauer would deny saying it.

The detective's eyes gleamed with a sick delight, as he was probably thinking the same thing. His diabolical stare laid bare the evil in his heart.

Cliff noticed something else—Jamie's body tensed, just for a fraction of a second. Cliff knew that look. He had seen it in her before—her measured breaths, her weight subtly shifting to her toes, the faint tension in her shoulders that only someone trained in violence would recognize.

She'd heard enough.

She was ready. She was always ready.

His pulse raced as he anticipated things coming to a head. He stood motionless to keep the detective calm. Bauer's gun wavered slightly, his eyes were hard and calculating, flicking between Cliff and Jamie.

The room felt too small, the air too heavy. Every twitch and sound seemed to echo like a warning.

But still, Jamie didn't make a move. She stood calmly like a predator waiting for its prey. After all, Bauer had a gun and knew how to use it. She had to choose her moment carefully.

Bauer, on the other hand, was growing impatient and enraged with every passing second. His smirk deepened, but there was a slight twitch in his jaw that betrayed his loss of control.

Perhaps Jamie's demeanor had caused him to pause. She didn't seem afraid of him at all. Her calmness was unnerving even to Cliff.

Bauer clearly was unsure what to do next. Cliff sensed his indecision. Could understand his dilemma.

He had to be careful, or his own plan would unravel. He had thought killing Grimes was the perfect crime, but it had resulted in several unknown complications beyond his control. He had somehow managed to come out of it unscathed, but not without some trepidation along the way.

This wasn't how he expected tonight to go either. He probably thought he'd sneak into their home and kill them in their sleep. Get assigned to investigate it and cover it up.

But they had confused him. He didn't know they knew about the affair. More importantly, he didn't know how much they knew or who else did as well.

Bauer kept looking at the stairs. Cliff knew why and his heart leapt in fear.

*Julia.*

An unknown for Bauer. She could be upstairs calling the police for all he knew.

Cliff could see all of this confusion processing in his mind as he shifted his weight nervously. His eyes flitted around like a cat in an alley filled with dogs, unsure what to do next.

Jamie's eyes met Cliff's for the briefest moment, and in them, Cliff saw the signal.

Whatever was about to happen was going to happen fast.

In a flash, she moved, faster than Cliff had ever seen.

She pivoted on the balls of her feet, launching herself at the detective with a speed almost inhuman. She twisted her body, one hand slamming into the detective's wrist with a force that sent his gun flying across the room.

Before he could react, Jamie spun around, hooking her leg behind his knee and yanking him off balance. The detective stumbled, his eyes wide with shock as Jamie's elbow crashed into the side of his head, momentarily stunning him.

He staggered but managed to maintain his balance. Bauer was a big man.

But Jamie wasn't done. Using her body weight, she took advantage of his momentum and pushed him to the ground.

She pounced with the precision of a seasoned killer, her hands a blur of controlled, lethal strikes. But she didn't intend to kill him, or he'd already be dead.

Bauer had to raise his hands to protect his head. The blows came so fast that he couldn't counter strike.

With his hands up, Jamie saw an opening and drove her knee into his chest. All the air escaped from his lungs, leaving him gasping. In one fluid motion, she flipped him onto his stomach, twisting his arm behind his back with a force that made him scream.

Cliff could only watch in awe, his own instincts momentarily frozen by the sheer speed and precision of her movements. It's like she choreographed the takedown in her mind before she acted.

He had always known Jamie was deadly but seeing her like this—a force of nature who could dismantle a man twice her size with ease—sent a chill running through his body. He couldn't help but marvel at her focus, her unflinching resolve as she twisted Bauer's arm into a grotesque angle that made Cliff wince.

His arm was useless now, broken in multiple places with joints separated from their sockets. The sound of flesh and tendons ripping sent a wave of nausea through Cliff's stomach.

She wasn't just skilled, she was extraordinary.

A flicker of gratitude washed over him as he at least had the presence of mind to retrieve Bauer's gun. Though Cliff pointed it in Bauer's direction, it seemed unnecessary as Jamie continued to subdue him with minimal effort.

"You're done, Bauer," Cliff asserted firmly. "You're not going to kill anyone else or cover up anything. It's over."

"Do you have any handcuffs?" Jamie asked, turning to Cliff. "And some rope?"

"Yes, I do," he replied. "They're in my office and garage. Are you okay here?"

She nodded, and he quickly retrieved the items along with his own gun.

With Cliff's help, Jamie forced Bauer onto a kitchen chair and secured his hands behind his back with a pair of cuffs. His arm hung limply by his side, completely useless. A skilled surgeon would need hours to piece it back together again. If he even could.

As the adrenaline faded, Cliff stepped back and took a deep breath. Jamie calmly secured Bauer to the chair with rope, her eyes burning with intensity despite her composed expression.

Julia suddenly appeared from the stairs, her eyes wide with shock at the unfolding scene in the living room. Cliff quickly filled her in and instructed her to call the police.

"No! Wait. I'll handle this myself," Jamie stated firmly.

Bauer's eyes were filled with pain and anger as he struggled against the tight bindings that restricted his movement. He managed to speak, but his voice was weak from the lack of breath. Cliff wouldn't be surprised if he had cracked ribs.

"Go ahead and call the police," he said defiantly. "You're all under arrest. You have the right to remain silent—"

"You're the one who's going to jail for a long time," Cliff said angrily.

"You ain't got nothing on me," Bauer said with a painful smirk.

"You broke into my house!" Cliff exclaimed.

"That's not how it happened," Bauer countered, regaining some confidence. "I've been investigating you two. I'm arresting all of you."

"On what charge?" Cliff demanded.

"Conspiracy to commit murder, accessory to murder, and obstruction of justice, for starters," Bauer replied, almost believing the words coming from his mouth. "Not to mention assaulting an officer of the law. Kidnapping. I'll think of a dozen more charges before I'm through with you."

Cliff shouted back. "You killed Grimes, not Allison."

"The three of you helped Allison kill him and then covered it up," Bauer accused with false conviction. "I had probable cause to enter your premises."

Cliff laughed incredulously. "Good luck with that argument."

But Cliff's laughter quickly turned to burning anger that erupted out of him. "You killed Grimes and tried to pin it on Allison, you piece of scum," Cliff practically shouted. "You tampered with the evidence, removing the autopsy report and deleting it from the coroner's computer, all because your wife was having an affair with him."

"You can't prove any of that!" Bauer protested.

"What did you do first?" Jamie interjected. "Hit Grimes over the head and crack his skull, or crush his windpipe?"

Bauer's eyes widened in shock. "How did you—?" He stopped himself before saying anything incriminating.

"You have nothing," he sneered.

"We have the autopsy report," Cliff countered.

Bauer visibly stiffened and his mouth opened, but no words came out.

Jamie's lips curled into a proud smirk. "And that's just the beginning."

Bauer quickly regained his composure. "There's my probable cause. You're the one who stole the autopsy report and deleted it from the computer. For all I know, you also hit him in the head with a mallet and crushed his windpipe."

Interesting that Bauer used the word mallet. Probably what he used as the murder weapon.

"I have an eyewitness who saw your wife at the marina," Jamie said coolly. "I also have copies of the text messages between your wife and Grimes. Did you know she told him she loved him? Would you like to read some of their explicit conversations?"

Bauer winced, a mixture of pain from his arm and his obvious broken heart.

"We've already seen those messages," Jamie continued. "We have them as well. The judge will definitely want to see them."

Jamie was clearly trying to provoke him now. And Cliff could see the problem she probably saw. They needed Bauer to confess or say something incriminating in order to build a stronger case against him.

"You better watch your back, lady," Bauer growled. "You can't pin this on me. I'll be back in business soon enough, and when I am, I'll make sure to kill you and dump your body in the ocean. And your friends too. I got to you once before, and I can do it again."

"You'll be going to jail for a long time, Bauer," Cliff interjected firmly.

"You have nothing on me. Who do you think they'll believe? You or me, Ford?"

Jamie pulled out her phone from her pocket. "I think they'll believe you."

She tapped something on her phone and Bauer's voice filled the room. Cliff couldn't believe it. She had recorded everything.

*How did she manage to do that?*

How did she remain calm enough to hit the record button on her phone despite facing a gun pointed at her?

When it got to the point where Bauer threatened to kill them, that's when he slumped in the chair in defeat.

"Who are you?" he asked.

"Who I am doesn't matter," Jamie said. "What matters is what I can do to you."

She got right in his face. Inches from him.

"You might get out on bail, Bauer, but know this. You come after me or my friends and you'll be the one who'll find himself in the bottom of the ocean. Unlike you, I don't make threats. I just carry them out."

Jamie had obviously turned off the recording. She wouldn't want that on tape. Without warning, she abruptly walked to the other side of the room and dialed a number on her phone.

Cliff's mind raced as he kept one eye on Bauer while he tried to process all this information. He felt the truth settle in. Allison's ordeal wasn't over—not by a long shot. But now, they had everything they needed to start turning the tide in her favor.

It'd take some doing to overturn the jury verdict, but Cliff would do everything he could to put the facts of the case together for Silver.

Jamie returned, her expression calm, her eyes blazing with quiet intensity. "It's handled," she whispered to Cliff and Julia. "I don't trust the local cops. I contacted someone I trust at the federal level. They'll make sure Bauer doesn't get away with this."

Cliff felt a weight lifted from his chest, the tension of the night slowly giving way to a sense of relief. Julia stepped closer, her fingers brushing his arm, grounding him in the moment. He put his arm around her, and she collapsed onto his shoulder.

"You really think they'll nail him?" she asked softly, her voice tinged with hope.

Jamie's lips curled into a faint, confident smile. "They will. And if they don't, I will."

"So, what now?" Cliff asked Jamie.

"We wrap this up properly. The truth is finally on our side, and Allison Mansfield deserves her freedom. Let's make sure she gets it."

"I feel like we are back in control, a step ahead instead of a step behind," Cliff said. "Allison's fate just took a dramatic and unexpected turn tonight."

Julia exhaled shakily. Her eyes widened as she realized something Cliff had forgotten about.

"I'm going to go check on Rita," she said, which reminded Cliff how close they came to disaster.

Rita was asleep upstairs in her bedroom, and they had an armed killer in their house.

*Thank God for Jamie.*

If she hadn't been there, no telling what might've happened.

# 21

*A week later*

The sun burned bright in the sky as Cliff and Julia sped down US-1, on their way to Key West, the road ahead flanked by turquoise waters on either side.

The Allison Mansfield case was finally behind them. Justice had prevailed in the end. Jamie's friends at the Feds had managed to extract a confession out of Detective Bauer that had led the judge to overturn the jury's verdict. Allison was exonerated, free to rebuild her life.

Cliff wasn't sure how he did it, but Alex somehow managed to make all of Allison's prenup agreements disappear. There wasn't a copy anywhere to be found, which meant she stood to inherit Grimes' entire estate. The mother would fight it, but an attorney in Silver's firm was handling it and liked their chances.

Once Allison was out of jail, a hefty sum appeared in their business bank account which more than compensated them for their time. Either from Jamie or from Allison.

Still, Cliff couldn't allow himself to relax. He had a worry that had been in the back of his mind for the past six weeks.

*Snowball.*

He'd never had a case that bugged him as much as this one and yet was so meaningless compared to the cases he normally worked on.

Over the past few weeks, when he wasn't thinking about Allison, he wracked his brain trying to figure out what the clever feline was up to. They confirmed with Mrs. Plumley that Snowball still left the house every morning at nine o'clock. Presumably to a neighbor's house where he got into her car for some strange reason and went somewhere.

*But where?*

Cliff wouldn't be satisfied until he solved that question.

Mrs. Plumley considered it kidnapping.

"I want that lady arrested!" she had said.

"The cat comes home every night!" Cliff countered. "It can't be considered kidnapping."

"She's taking Snowball against his will."

"He looked pretty content to me sitting in the passenger seat of that car," Cliff said, which was the wrong thing to say to Mrs. Plumley.

"Whose side are you on?" she practically shouted.

"All I'm saying is—"

"Are you going to solve this crime or do I need to find someone else? I've already paid you ten thousand dollars, and I have nothing to show for it."

Julia had to smooth things over.

"Sometimes these things take time," she said in her disarming voice. "We're coming down this week and we're going to figure things out. We told you that we were working on a murder case. That's over now. We can give you our full attention."

"You better hurry or I fear we might have another murder on our hands."

Cliff wasn't sure if she was referring to Snowball's potential murder or to the neighbor's if Mrs. Plumley got her hands on the woman. Either way, they were running out of time. The mystery needed to be solved right away.

For Cliff's sanity as much as anything.

His plan was to confront the mystery woman when she returned home later that afternoon. They couldn't get to Key West in time to find her in the morning, so the plan was to arrive before lunch, then stake out the street sometime after two. The woman probably wouldn't return with Snowball until closer to five, but Cliff wasn't going to take any chances.

"Afternoon is better, anyway," Cliff had said. "She'll be coming home. We'll find out which house she's in and confront her then. If we try to catch her in the morning, she could just drive away."

"What do you think they're up to?" Julia had asked.

"I have no idea," Cliff said honestly, with as much frustration behind the words as he could muster.

"Do you think it's something illegal, like Mrs. Plumley believes?"

"What? You think Snowball is an accomplice to a crime? That the woman is using him to rob banks or something?"

"No. I'm just confused. I want to know what they're doing."

"We'll get to the bottom of it today. We'll *purr-sue* every lead," Cliff said, with a wide smile on his face. "Get the pun? Purr-sue."

Julia rolled her eyes. "I get it."

Cliff felt a satisfied smirk settle over his face at the witty pun that he had thought of a few weeks before and had waited until the right time to fit it into the conversation. He'd never let Julia know he hadn't thought of it off the top of his head.

He grinned to himself. Humor was his weapon of choice against the ridiculous, and this case was as ridiculous as they came.

"Do you ever get the sense that we attract chaos?" Julia asked. "I thought when we

moved from Chicago, things were going to get quieter."

Cliff shot her a sideways glance. "I told you we shouldn't have taken this case. It's just a cat for goodness' sake."

"Hey, Snowball isn't just any cat. Do I need to remind you that she's paying us twenty thousand dollars to find this cat, and I promised her we'd deliver? What if we can't?"

Cliff grumbled but couldn't suppress a smile. "We'll solve the case. If it's the last thing I do. We need to stay *paw-sitive*."

Julia let out a groan.

He nudged her with his right hand. Playfully poking her in the ribs.

"Get it? Pawwwww . . sitive. A cat has paws."

"I got it."

"You didn't laugh."

"That's because it wasn't funny."

She was trying not to laugh. Julia bit her lip and looked out the window in the other direction so he couldn't see her smiling.

They drove in companionable silence for a while, the miles ticking by as the shimmering waters of the Keys surrounded them. Julia broke the quiet again, her tone somewhat serious.

"Okay, okay, but what if we never find him? What do we tell Mrs. Plumley?"

"We'll tell her he's been running a tiki bar on the beach."

Julia chuckled. "A tiki bar, huh? What's it called? The Pussy Cat Lounge?"

"Yeah. Drinks served with a side of *cat-titude*."

They both let out a good laugh that eased the tension further. By the time they reached Key West, Cliff's mood had lightened considerably, though he still felt the pressing urgency of unfinished business.

Julia, ever the planner, suggested they make the most of their time by visiting *Hemingway House*. It's the only tourist attraction on her list they hadn't gotten to the last time they visited Key West.

"You can't come to Key West and not see Hemingway's place. Besides, maybe the cats there will inspire us. Maybe one of them can tell us how to find Snowball."

Cliff agreed. They had a couple of hours to kill. They were met by a perky woman at a ticket booth outside the house. She asked if they wanted to pay extra for the tour, and Cliff immediately said yes, knowing that's what Julia would prefer even though he liked to roam around an attraction himself without being tied down.

The tour began around back by the swimming pool, where six-toed cats lounged like royalty. Their guide regaled the group with tales of Hemingway's love for felines. Cliff couldn't help but admire the sheer audacity of the cats, as if they knew they were as much a part of history as the man himself.

Inside the back house, the tour meandered through Hemingway's writing studio and library, then to the main house, starting in the dining room and kitchen, living room, and finally upstairs to the master bedroom. Cliff was about to tune out the guide's description of the furniture when Julia gasped.

"Cliff," she whispered urgently, grabbing his arm. "Look!"

There, stretched across the crisp white linens of the four-poster bed, was a white cat. The cat blinked lazily at the group of tourists snapping photos, utterly unbothered by the commotion.

"No way," Cliff muttered, his jaw dropping.

"It *is* him!" Julia said. "Look at the collar. That's Snowball."

The guide noticed their reaction and raised an eyebrow. "You know Snowball?"

Cliff nodded slowly. "Yeah, he belongs to a client of ours."

Her eyes widened.

"That cat was stolen," Cliff said.

"That's impossible! Marcy brings him to work with her every day. She says he's a stray she adopted. He's become a bit of a celebrity here. Did you know that Hemingway had a white cat named Snowball?"

"We need to talk to this Marcy," Cliff said sternly.

"You already have. She's the one working at the ticket counter. She took your money."

"You stay here," Cliff said to Julia. "Don't let Snowball out of your sight!"

When Snowball heard his name, he looked up at Cliff and Julia. His face flashed a startled look of recognition. Without warning, he jumped down.

Cliff lunged for him.

Snowball darted under the table, his tail flicking like a white blur. Cliff scrambled to his knees, reaching out, but Snowball skittered sideways, dodging him by inches.

"Stop that cat!" Cliff yelled, rising to his feet and knocking into a chair.

The tour guide let out a scream. The rest of the tour let out a collective gasp.

Julia leapt into action as well, cutting off Snowball's escape route toward the staircase. "I've got this side covered!"

Snowball paused, his ears flattening, then veered right, slipping through the legs of a startled tourist.

"Excuse me!" Julia shouted, sidestepping the confused bystander.

Cliff bolted after the cat, who dashed through a doorway into what appeared to be a parlor filled with antique furniture and velvet drapes. Snowball leapt onto a side table, scattering a stack of brochures and knocking over a lamp that crashed to the floor. He bounded toward the top of an ornate bookshelf.

Cliff reached for him, but Snowball launched himself through the air, landing gracefully on a chandelier.

"You've got to be kidding me," Cliff muttered, watching as the cat swayed back and forth, his eyes glinting mischievously.

"Careful!" Julia called, running in behind him. "This place looks expensive."

"Yeah, no kidding," Cliff said, jumping to grab Snowball as the cat leapt again, this time onto the staircase banister. He slid halfway down before springing off, landing with a soft thud on the plush carpet at the bottom of the stairs.

"He's heading for the lobby!" Julia yelled, taking off at full speed down the steps two at a time. Cliff followed close behind.

Julia spotted Snowball immediately and pointed. The cat zigzagged across the floor, his paws skidding on the polished surface. They scrambled after him, dodging furniture and guests. Footsteps echoed through the room, adding to the chaos.

Near the lobby, Snowball made a sharp turn and slipped into a staff-only hallway. Julia caught the door just before it swung shut, and Cliff followed her inside.

"He's cornered now," Cliff said, breathing hard.

They rounded the corner to find Snowball perched smugly on a high shelf, his tail swishing. He stared down at them, his green eyes gleaming with victory.

"Great," Julia said. "How do you plan to get him down?"

Before Cliff could answer, Snowball leapt down onto a rolling laundry cart and pushed off with his back legs, sending it careening toward another door.

"Not again!" Cliff bellowed as he and Julia raced after the cart, only to find it empty when they reached it.

A soft *meow* from the nearby open window told them everything. Snowball was outside now, slipping into thick hedges by the parking lot.

"Snowball!" Cliff called, panting.

Julia shook her head in disbelief. "That cat is better at evading you than half the criminals you've chased."

Cliff groaned, watching the last flicker of Snowball's tail disappear into the greenery. "This isn't over."

The sound of heavy boots echoed down the corridor just as Cliff and Julia emerged from the staff hallway, still catching their breath. A burly security guard with a stern face and crossed arms blocked their path. His navy-blue uniform stretched over his broad frame, and the radio on his belt crackled faintly.

"What do you think you're doing?" the guard demanded, his voice sharp.

"We're chasing a cat," Cliff said, holding up his hands in a gesture of surrender.

"A cat?" The guard's eyebrows shot up. "I'll have you know that you're trespassing in a restricted area and destroying property?"

Julia stepped forward, her tone calm but firm. "We're private investigators. Snowball belongs to one of our clients. We believe he was stolen."

The guard narrowed his eyes. "I don't care who you are. You've got no business here. Leave now, or I'll call the police—and you'll be paying for that lamp."

"I'm not paying for the lamp. The cat is the one—" Julie cut him off with a quick glance.

Cliff clenched his jaw. "Look, we don't want any trouble. All we're asking for is a conversation with Marcy, the woman at the ticket counter. She's the one who brought Snowball here."

The guard's eyes flicked toward the lobby, his suspicion unabated. "I'll take you to her. But don't try anything. One wrong move, and you're going to jail."

Cliff bristled. The guard was obviously a bit power hungry, taking his job a little too seriously.

"You don't understand, sir. Snowball ran outside. If we don't catch him now, we might lose him again."

The guard's radio buzzed, and a voice called his name. He ignored it, glaring at Cliff. "I don't care if the queen's corgi ran outside. You're done here."

Julia raised her hands in a placating gesture. "Please, we don't need to make this a bigger deal than it is. Marcy might have no idea Snowball belongs to someone else. If we can clear this up with her, we'll be out of your hair. And we'll pay for that lamp."

The guard hesitated, his jaw locked tightly. "Five minutes. That's all you've got. Then I want you to leave the property."

"Deal." Cliff gave him a tight nod.

"She's at the counter." The guard jerked his thumb toward the lobby. "Make it quick."

As they hurried past him, Cliff muttered, "This cat is more trouble than he's worth."

"Good thing trouble is your specialty." Julia's lips curled into a smirk.

Cliff chuckled but his mind raced. They might've solved the mystery, but now they had a bigger problem.

Where was Snowball?

# 22

Cliff dreaded the thought of having to face Mrs. Plumley and break the news that her beloved cat, Snowball, had once again run off. This time, it seemed like he might be gone for good. The cunning feline had outsmarted them at every turn, and Cliff couldn't make any promises about when or if he would return.

He thought the mystery was solved when they saw Snowball lounging luxuriously at Ernest Hemingway's house on his bed. He looked as if he belonged there, almost like he was channeling the author's own pet cat named Snowball.

As soon as Cliff took a step forward, the cat bolted, and they were led on a frantic chase throughout the house. Onlookers laughed and cheered as the feline ducked under tables and leapt onto windowsills. Finally, Snowball escaped through an open window, disappearing into the sunny streets of Key West.

They questioned Marcy, who lived near Mrs. Plumley and brought Snowball to work with her every day. She seemed genuinely shocked to learn that Snowball had an owner and that she had hired a private investigator to find him.

"I had no idea anyone was looking for him," she stuttered anxiously, wringing her hands. "I found him wandering around my house one day. The name on his collar is Snowball, like Hemingway's cat, so I started bringing him to work with me. He seemed to love it here."

Cliff sighed. "Did you ever think to check if he had an owner?"

"I tried following him a few times, but he's too clever—always one step ahead," she defended herself. "I thought he was a stray."

"Have you ever seen a stray cat that was treated as well as that one? He's even more pampered than my wife," Cliff quipped.

Julia gave him a sharp look and muttered loud enough for Cliff to hear, "That's an understatement."

Ignoring their playful banter, Marcy showed her distress at this unexpected news. "Am I in trouble?" she asked nervously.

"Not yet," Cliff replied sternly. "But if we don't find Snowball and return him to Mrs. Plumley, she might think he's been kidnapped."

"Kidnapped? Oh no! That's not what I meant to do," Marcy exclaimed fearfully. "If there was a phone number on his collar, I would have called. I swear."

Cliff almost felt sorry for her. "I believe you," he reassured her, softening his tone. He had to admit that a collar without contact information was not very useful.

She clearly had no malicious intentions. If anything, she seemed just as attached to Snowball as Mrs. Plumley.

Her eyes suddenly widened. "Wait," she said. "What do you mean he's missing?"

Cliff explained the situation and told her where Snowball had escaped through the window. Marcy seemed genuinely horrified that Snowball was no longer in the house.

After scouring the area for almost an hour, they finally admitted defeat and concluded that Snowball was not hiding anywhere on the premises.

"Do you think he'll be able to find his way back home?" Cliff asked Marcy.

"I'm not sure. He's a smart cat," Marcy replied.

"Don't I know it."

"But I don't know that he's street smart. He's been riding in the car with me every day. I'm not sure he knows his way back home."

"We should go tell his owner that he's missing," Cliff said with resignation in his voice.

"I'll keep looking," Marcy said, matching his soberness, trying to hold back her tears. "Maybe he'll come back here. I'll make sure everyone keeps an eye out for him."

The drive to Mrs. Plumley's house was tense and quiet, both Cliff and Julia scanned the streets intently for any sign of white fur.

As they pulled into Mrs. Plumley's driveway, Cliff's heart started to race. He wasn't sure why he was so nervous. This was a case of a missing cat, not a high-profile murder he was trying to solve. As a detective, he had experienced many difficult conversations with family members about their loved ones being victims of crime, and this situation made him feel similarly anxious.

Julia rang the doorbell, and within moments, the elderly woman appeared with a warm smile.

"Come in, come in," she urged them inside. The familiar scent of old furniture and pumpkin-scented candles greeted them.

She led them to the living room where Cliff instinctively looked at the bay window, hoping to see Snowball lounging there. But there was no sign of him, and his heart sank a little.

"I hope you've solved this little mystery," Mrs. Plumley said, her tone cheerful but tinged with curiosity.

Cliff and Julia shared a quick glance, silently debating who should tell her the truth.

"We have some good news and some bad news," Julia began, her voice steady but gentle.

Mrs. Plumley's smile faltered. "Let's start with the good news. I like to see the glass as half full."

Julia took a deep breath. "We discovered where Snowball has been going."

Mrs. Plumley leaned forward, her interest piqued. "Oh? And what has that little rascal been up to?"

Julia grinned. "It turns out, Snowball is quite the celebrity."

"Celebrity?" Mrs. Plumley's penciled-in eyebrows shot up in surprise.

"He's been the main attraction at the Hemingway House for several months now. Can you believe we found him lounging on Hemingway's bed like he owned the place?"

Mrs. Plumley gasped, her hand flying to her chest in shock. "Really? I had no idea," she exclaimed.

Julia added, "He's probably the most photographed cat in all of Florida."

Mrs. Plumley smile widened, a mix of amusement and pride evident on her face. "Did I ever mention that I actually met Ernest Hemingway once? My husband introduced me to him at a party back in 1961, a few weeks before he passed away. He was quite an eccentric man, to say the least."

"The tour guide mentioned he was," Julia said with a smile.

"He was very kind to us and told me all about his beloved cats, including one named Snowball who was his pride and joy. That's why our first cat was also named Snowball; this is actually our fifth one now."

Cliff couldn't help but suppress a smile.

She chuckled and added, "But none of the previous Snowballs gave me as much trouble as this one." Her expression turned thoughtful and suddenly she gasped, "Wait a minute ... do you think this Snowball could be a reincarnation of Papa Hemingway or possibly related to him somehow? That would explain his fascination with spending every day at the Hemingway House."

Julia quickly shot Cliff a warning look not to say anything, and before he could respond, the doorbell rang. Both Cliff and Julia jumped while Mrs. Plumley shuffled over to answer it.

A moment later, they heard her exclaim, "Snowball! My little angel!"

She came back into the room cradling the cat in her arms as he purred contentedly snuggling against her neck. Behind her was Marcy, looking both relieved and slightly embarrassed.

"I found him wandering back toward the Hemingway House," she said quietly to Cliff and Julia. "It looks like he was trying to find his way back."

Cliff made the introductions, deciding to frame Marcy's role in the best possible light.

"Mrs. Plumley, this is Marcy. She's been taking care of Snowball. She works at the Hemingway House and has been giving him all kinds of adventures."

Mrs. Plumley beamed. "Well, bless you, dear. I can't thank you enough. You've been so good to him."

Marcy smiled shyly. "He's a special cat. I'm sorry for any trouble I caused."

"Nonsense! You can take him to work whenever you like. As long as he comes home at night."

Mrs. Plumley insisted she stay and sit on the couch next to her. Snowball stretched lazily and nestled into Marcy's lap. The two women cooed over him, their bond solidified by their shared affection for the mischievous feline. Mrs. Plumley insisted that Marcy have dinner with her. It looked like they were becoming fast friends.

Cliff declined the invitation. "We should be going. If we leave now, we can get back to Miami before dark."

"I can't thank you enough," she said, effusively. Even giving Cliff a hug which Snowball didn't like. He hissed at him.

She led Cliff and Julia to the door after writing them a check for ten thousand dollars. Cliff was relieved to get out of there and to finally put the case behind them.

"Send me the bill for your expenses," Mrs. Plumley said as they stepped outside. "And thank you for all you've done for me."

Before they could get off the porch, she stopped them. "Julia, dear, you never told me the bad news," Mrs. Plumley said, her voice light and curious.

Julia waved dismissively. "Not important now."

Mrs. Plumley smiled widely. "Okay. Toodle-doo! Drive safely."

As they walked to the car, Cliff muttered, "I'm glad this is over. I thought you said it was going to be easy."

"I was wrong. When have you ever had an 'easy case'?"

Cliff couldn't argue with that.

# 23

Three weeks had passed, and Cliff was back to feeling bored. No phone calls, no new clients since their return from Key West. He wondered if they would ever have another case to solve.

He leaned back in his chair, twirling a pen between his fingers as he looked around the silent office. The fluorescent lights buzzed softly above, accompanied by the ticking of the clock on the wall. The faint sounds blared in his ear, taunting him, reminding him how much he missed the thrill of a continual stream of murder investigations back in Chicago.

After successfully cracking two important cases with Julia, he desperately craved more action.

Meanwhile, Julia focused on organizing some files for future cases, her forehead scrunched in concentration. She had always been the more structured one, finding order in chaos while Cliff preferred being away from the office, investigating.

"Do you think we'll get another case soon?" Cliff finally broke the silence.

Julia looked up from her work and flashed him a reassuring smile. "I'm sure something will come our way. We need to be patient."

"Patience is not my strong suit," Cliff admitted.

She waved a flyer in front of him. "I saw this ad for a billboard. We could advertise our services on it. I've already got the caption: 'We'll find your missing cat!'"

"Don't even think about it!" Cliff exclaimed.

"Mrs. Plumley promised to give us a good reference," Julia said.

"I'm done chasing cats," Cliff stated firmly.

"Don't knock it. We got two trips to Key West out of it, plus twenty thousand dollars and expenses paid. And we successfully solved the case. That's what you call a win-win situation. I'd take four more cases just like it."

They settled into a familiar monotony for the rest of the morning and Cliff tried to find things to keep himself busy. Something Julia had no trouble with as it seemed she was always busy, both at home and in the office.

A few hours after lunch, an unexpected guest interrupted them. A man, who appeared to be in his eighties, entered through the door with a stiff gate and slightly hunched shoulders. He scanned the room nervously as he made his way inside. His hair was dyed and immaculately groomed, his jacket smart and shirt starched and pressed, and although his tie looked like it was from another era, he clearly had taken great care to knot it.

"I'm looking for Cliff Ford and Julie ... uh ... Julia," his heavy British accent, weak and trembling, made Cliff wonder if the man should be on the streets of Miami alone.

"That's us," Cliff stood to greet him and offered his hand. "How can we help you?"

The man shook his hand briefly but with surprising strength. "Well, I need an investigator. A friend of mine, Penelope Plumley, referred me to you. She speaks highly of your work."

Cliff immediately became wary. Did this man also have a missing cat?

"What's your name?" Julia asked, standing by Cliff's side and leading the visitor to a chair in front of Cliff's desk.

"Can I get you something to drink?" she added kindly.

"No thank you," he replied. "My name is Cuthbert Elliot."

"What a *brilliant* name," Julia said, slipping effortlessly into a faux British brogue. "Positively regal. Very stiff upper lip and all that, isn't it?"

During their private moments, Julia sometimes spoke to Cliff in a convincing British accent.

The man nodded and smiled with fake amusement.

"What brings you to us today, Mr. Elliot?" Julia asked. "You said that Mrs. Plumley referred you. Do you have a missing cat?"

Cliff braced himself for an answer he would dread hearing.

The man chuckled, "I wouldn't be caught dead with one of those despicable creatures."

"What is it then?" Cliff asked, feeling a sense of relief.

"Mrs. Plumley told me that you specialize in finding lost pets."

The tension returned. "We don't specialize in—"

"That is one area of our expertise," Julia said, cutting off Cliff's protest. "One of many. What kind of pet do you have?"

Cuthbert hesitated. "Um ... It's my bird. He's gone missing."

Cliff shook his head in disbelief. "Your bird?"

The man nodded solemnly, as serious as an astronaut preparing for liftoff.

"My pigeon, to be more precise. His name is Casper."

"Like the ghost?" Julia said.

"Yes. Cas-per ..." His voice cracked. He was clearly torn up inside even talking about it.

"Did someone steal him?" Cliff asked, mildly intrigued and raising his eyebrow slightly.

He wasn't interested in finding a missing pet, but a stolen pet might get his investigative juices flowing and add an element of danger to the search.

Cuthbert shook his head. "I'm rather embarrassed. I was cleaning his cage and forgot to close the bedroom window. He flew out."

"He flew out the window!" Cliff exclaimed with exasperation. "And now you want us to find him! How am I supposed to do that? There must be a billion pigeons in Miami alone. He could be anywhere."

Cuthbert shook his head.

"It won't be as hard as you think. I'd do it myself, but I'm not physically able."

"Why do you think it'll be so easy?"

"Casper is a unique pigeon. An albino marvel—a beacon of avian elegance."

His British sophistication came through as he spoke with pride about his bird.

"Being an albino, he's completely white with pink eyes. It's a rarity, as less than one percent of pigeons are born albino. He'll be easy to recognize."

"But he could be anywhere," Cliff argued, throwing his hands in the air. "I wouldn't even know where to start looking. For all I know, he could have flown south for the winter."

Cuthbert gave Cliff a disapproving look.

"Pigeons don't migrate, sir. They are homebodies and like to stay close to their nests. I would expect someone who specializes in pet searches to know that."

"We don't—"

"What my husband means," Julia said, cutting in smoothly, "is that pigeons may not be our usual case, but finding what's lost, that's what we do best. I'm sure we can help you find Casper."

Cuthbert looked suspiciously at Cliff, who returned the same level of distrust. The idea of finding one bird among millions seemed impossible, even if Casper was still in the area.

So many potential obstacles flashed into his mind at once. What if he found the bird? How would he catch it? He couldn't even catch Snowball on the ground. What was to stop Casper from flying away and making him start the search all over again?

"Mrs. Plumley mentioned your usual fee," the man said. "I'll double it. Money is not an issue."

"That sounds fair," Julia replied with a smile.

Cliff's body jolted in surprise, nearly causing him to fall out of his chair. Was this man seriously offering them $40,000 to look for a lost bird?

Cliff wanted to turn down the offer immediately for several reasons. Mainly, he didn't want his reputation as a private investigator to include fleecing senior citizens out of their money. Before he could voice his objection, the man pulled out a photo of Casper and showed it to Julia who couldn't contain her excitement.

"He's so beautiful! What a lovely white color," she gushed.

She handed the photo to Cliff, but he only gave it a quick glance. Cuthbert noticed and looked at Cliff with disdain.

"I cannot stress enough how important it is for you to find him," the man said with a serious tone. "Casper is worth a lot of money."

"How much is 'a lot'?" Cliff asked skeptically.

"One point four million dollars."

Cliff froze, the pen he'd been tapping on the desk slipped from his fingers. "Did you say *million*? For a pigeon?"

This had to be some kind of joke.

"As I mentioned before, they are extremely rare. I've been offered one million dollars for him before, but I would never sell him."

Cliff pulled out his phone and quickly searched for the value of Albino pigeons while Cuthbert and Julia chatted excitedly. To his surprise, Cuthbert was right. Albino pigeons were valued at over a million dollars. He could hardly believe it.

"Well done, Cuthbert," Julia praised with enthusiasm. "You've secured the best investigators in Miami."

Cliff slumped back in his chair but stayed quiet about his doubts.

At least this case gave him an opportunity for some investigative work. The high value involved raised his level of interest significantly. He planned on searching the beach and boardwalk for a few days. If they found nothing, he would refund the fee.

After the man paid them half the agreed upon fee, he left.

Cliff let out a groan as soon as he was out of earshot.

Julia shot Cliff a disapproving look. "A moment ago, you were complaining about not having any cases. Now you have one that will take you out of the office. You'll get paid to stroll the beach, soak up the sun, and spot a million-dollar pigeon. It's practically a vacation. How many people can say they've done that?"

"I suppose," Cliff replied begrudgingly. "But it's not going to be as easy as you make it sound."

"A white pigeon in Miami?" Julia said, grinning widely. "Practically a spotlight on wings. I'll make up some flyers. We'll spread them around town. You'll be a hero by Thursday."

Cliff was aware of what was about to happen. He knew himself too well. The moment he got involved, the case would consume him—every lead, every dead end, every sleepless night chasing a pigeon through Miami.

It'd drive him crazy.

And that's just how he liked it.

Thank you for purchasing this novel from best-selling author, Terry Toler. As an additional thank you, Terry wants to give you a free gift.

Sign up for:

*Updates*
*New Releases*
*Announcements*

At terrytoler.com

We'll send you an eBook, *The Book Club*, a Cliff Hangers novella, free of charge.

# READ MORE BOOKS FROM TERRY TOLER

Jamie Austen Thrillers

Read all the Jamie Austen Thrillers. They must be good.
They've been number one on Amazon in ten different countries.
Click on the link below.

THE JAMIE AUSTEN THRILLERS (12 book series)
Kindle Edition (amazon.com)

https://amzn.to/3vmPUy7

## Cliff Hangers Mystery Series

Who wants to read a good mystery? We've got you covered! Read the Cliff Hangers where homicide detective, Cliff Ford, solves crimes in Chicago, with help from his wife Julia. These books have everything Terry Toler is known for. Page turning suspense, a hint of romance, and an ending you won't see coming.

The Cliff Hangers Mystery Series (4 book series)
Kindle Edition (amazon.com)

https://amzn.to/36WX3go

# About Terry

Terry Toler is an Amazon international # 1 best-selling and award-winning author. He writes clean fiction with a message and life-changing nonfiction. He's a public speaker, entrepreneur, and has authored more than forty books.

Sign up for his newsletter where you'll get free stuff, exclusive content, and news of releases and promotions. He can be followed at terrytoler.com.

If you like his books, please take a few minutes to leave a review on Amazon. We really appreciate it. It helps draw more readers to his books. Thanks!

www.ingramcontent.com/pod-product-compliance
Lightning Source LLC
Chambersburg PA
CBHW020327260626
47156CB00004B/1416